LONDON HORROR STORIES

TONY WALKER

CONTENTS

INTRODUCTION

This collection is called *London Horror Stories*, but in fact it contains a few ghost stories. What is the difference between a horror story and a ghost story? They both contain supernatural elements to be sure, but a horror story generally has a bad outcome for the main character, while a ghost story can turn out well.

Ghost stories tend to have a moral message. Horror stories can have a moral message too of course. The message in a horror story is often don't poke your nose where it doesn't belong and a tale about the dangers of curiosity, which of course killed the cat and many other folk.

Ghost stories are often about the ghost having a purpose in contacting the living, either for revenge or sometimes to help the living. The two obvious ghost stories in this collection: *The Golden Saxophone* and *Tick-Tock* are definitely along those lines. *Bad Times in Little Venice* and *The Lift* are just a bit horrible, while in *Gematria*, the character suffers a fate she definitely doesn't deserve. I hope you don't hate me too much for that.

I wrote this collection hot, or at least lukewarm, on the heels of my previous book *Cumbrian Ghost Stories*. I am very attracted to stories with a sense of place and I like to locate the stories in specific locations, often places I know and love.

When I lived in London, I had a flatmate called Andy. Andy used to mysteriously go out on his own every Sunday, not telling me where he was going. This was long ago in the days of the *London A-Z*. Eventually, I asked him what he was doing. I had hesitated in case it was something sinister, but it turned out he used to get the A-Z, roll dice and then go to wherever in London the dice told him to go. I liked that.

When I come back to London, I tend to wander the villages, and you will probably guess my favourites from the frequency they turn up in the stories.

I also notice a lot of nurses, doctors and other medical folk in the stories and a lot of characters who like psychedelic rock. I wonder why?

I hope that does not detract from your pleasure. If you like wandering mysterious London I would recommend you read books by Iain Sinclair and the newish book by Merlin Coverley *Occult London*.

You can get hold of me via my other books, listed at the back, or listen to me tell classic ghost stories on the Classic Ghost Stories Podcast, which you can find via your favourite podcast player or at www.ghostpod.org

I hope you enjoy the stories, and if you do, please leave a review!
Tony Walker

THE SHADOW OF THE RIPPER

Rain lashed the dreary London street, forcing Molly McGlave to shelter behind the soot-stained bricks of an alley wall. It was late; past 2 a.m. A gas lamp burned halfway down Durward Street and Molly was thinking she'd make her way back to Crossingham's doss house. She rustled in the cloth pouch she kept inside her shirt and took out the grubby coins. Gazing at them in the poor light, nestled in the palm of her hand, she saw had threepence; if she got one more punter, she could stop in at the Blind Beggar's lock-in and buy herself a gin or two.

As suddenly as it came, the rain stopped. Though the deluge had ceased, water still dripped from faded signs and gurgled down broken drainpipes. The rain had flushed onto the roadway, clearing away some of the shit that lay there. Molly shivered and pulled her poor shawl tighter round her. It was so cold you wouldn't think it was still supposed to be summer, even if it were past midnight.

She heard a tap-tap and thought maybe this was her chance and she stepped out of Buck's Row, but it was no punter, it was a copper with his bull's eye lantern. She dipped back into the alley, but he saw her. He yelled, 'Ere, girl, don't be lurking in the shadows. Time for you to get back home; pretend you're a decent woman keeping regular hours.'

'Too late for that!' she said, her voice sounding very Irish even to her.

He was good natured. 'Go on with you now. Get to bed; I don't want you coming to harm on these dark streets.'

'I can look after myself,' Molly said, but all the same, she made as if to walk down Winthrop Street. When the policeman had gone on his way, the sound of his heavy steps fading into the distance, she ducked back down Buck's Row.

She was parched. She really fancied a gin. Being drunk helped with sleeping in the doss house with its farting and snoring and coughing residents each and every night. A drink, then, and if the Blind Beggar had no lock in tonight, maybe the Frying Pan would be open?

But she had enough money for her doss, but no more than that. She sighed. Pity she couldn't find a punter to help her get gin, but it was late and she was tired. She gazed around the wet street. Nobody much about, though at least the rain was holding off. Just the drip drip drip, of draining water. The gurgle of it in the gutters. A little gusting breeze blowing down the street, chilling her further.

Then there was an odd noise. She started; a fluttering like the wings of a trapped bird, and a smell: a strange smell, like hot metal. She looked all around. Where were they coming from? The noise got louder: fluttering and rustling, and the smell more acrid. It was really like metal burning. Like heated iron in the blacksmith's shops. Like a furnace. Molly stopped, alone on the street in the small hours of the London night, and she felt afraid.

The noise and smell were all around her. She turned, instantly aware of an unseen gaze. Spinning on the soles of her broken-down boots, she saw a man up close behind her. Where had he come from? How could he have got so close up to her without her noticing? He didn't speak, tall and dark, a top-hat on his head, a heavy black overcoat down to his ankles. She couldn't make out his shadowed face with the gaslight burning behind him.

He watched her, silently.

She swallowed. Still, this was what she wanted: a punter. He must be a punter. What else would a man be doing on these streets at night? From his garb, he looked like he was decked out for a night on the town, though everything was long since shut. Maybe he had been looking to finish his fun with a woman, and she thought why not a pretty young Irish lady like herself? Still she hesitated.

She opened her mouth to speak, but there was something about this man she didn't like. All the girls got a sense of danger, the blokes who would be nice, the blokes who would be rough, the blokes who were just bastards from beginning to end.

The man waited for her to speak. She pursed her lips. She was going to call over to him to ask him if he wanted any business. She told herself another threepence and she'd be in the lock-in. If she got lucky, maybe somebody would buy her a drink and then if she threw in her doss money she'd be in the pub till dawn and tomorrow was another day.

This bloke would probably be quick. They could nip down Buck's Row.

But still something told her to be silent. To turn and hurry away. Her mouth opened, lips dry despite the rain. And then she spun round on her shabby boots and ran, lifting her skirts with both hands so she could run faster. She'd do without the extra gin.

And then she saw Mary Nichols coming towards her the other way. Nichols was a prostitute like herself, and she was dead drunk. Molly saw that from the outset. Though she was called Mary, for some reason she preferred Polly.

'Iya, Molly, you Fenian 'ore! 'ow ya doin'?'

Polly didn't wait for Molly's reply. She gave a bold wink. 'I got my doss money three times today, and I spent it. I got to get some more.'

Molly stopped, still mindful of the man not far away. She said, 'Drink'll be the death of you, Polly. Come with me and get to bed.'

'Nah, I don't take charity.' She smirked and rolled, her shoulder stooped with drink. A dirty cackle broke from her. 'Well, I do. But if I could just get one more job, then I'd be sorted.'

Molly went to take Polly's arm, but Polly shook her off. 'Just one more job.' Then she laughed. 'Maybe two.' She could hardly stand. She lurched back against the wall, steadying herself with her hand.

Molly was more insistent. 'Come with me now, Poll. Come on.'

Polly knocked her arm away, suddenly aggressive. Molly knew how quickly drunks could turn from friendly to fighting you. She didn't need that. With a snort, Molly said, 'Suit yourself, Poll, but don't say I never offered.'

Polly laughed. 'I'll be fine, you Irish tart. Fuck off now and leave me be.' Then she staggered on the way Molly had come from. Molly stopped and called. 'Don't go that way. There's a man.'

Over her shoulder, Mary yelled. 'That's what's I'm after, you stupid cow!'

'Polly!' Molly called again, but Polly Nichols had staggered off into the darkness. Molly heard her singing drunkenly as she went. The clatter of her boots echoing down the empty street.

Then it started to rain again. Hosing it down, bouncing off the cobbles. It rained and rained and rained, and it had not stopped by the time she got to her lodgings.

It was after 11 next morning when Molly woke at the doss house. Molly had a single room with a weekly change of bed linen. Her windows had to be open at 10 am to air them according to the rules, but she slept through as she always did. She made her way to the communal kitchen to see what scraps she could filch from those who called her friend. In there, she met John Dove, a sly man, a burglar by trade. He said, 'I 'eard one o' yours got it last night.' He drew a dirty finger across his dirty neck with a sound that signified the cutting of a throat.

It was not so rare that a prostitute was killed, but she thought she'd have heard something in the Frying Pan when she'd been in earlier yesterday, unless it had happened later.

'Who?' Molly said, taking a piece of cheese from an unguarded plate. The cheese was hard and green, but better than nothing.

'That Mary Nichols.'

'Polly? Get away with ye,' Molly said, swallowing the morsel of hard cheese, but she shuddered anyway. The sense of foreboding returned. 'I seen her last night. She was fine, so she was.'

'She weren't fine in the end. They found 'er down Buck's Row. Cut open real bad.'

Dove enjoyed seeing the alarm on her face. Still a good Catholic girl, Molly crossed herself. It was the man she'd seen that had done it; she was sure of it. The man who'd appeared from nowhere. It could have been her. Her throat tightened. 'Cut open, you say?'

''E done it like 'e was a butcher, or a surgeon. You girls better be careful. They ain't caught 'im.' John Dove raised a warning finger. 'Sure as eggs is eggs 'e'll kill again.'

Molly remembered the copper. Maybe she should find him and tell him she'd seen the man? But it was dark, and she could only give a vague description, and it wasn't her business away. And on top of that, when had she ever trusted a policeman? And why would they listen to a common street whore? And an Irish street whore at that. Lots of reasons to do nothing. But she was sweating. She leaned on the table. She knew it could have so easily been her cut open real bad and left dead in an alley like a bag of bones. She felt faint.

'Did you just nick my cheese you fucking Irish bitch?' The harsh Cockney voice of Annie Chapman, Dark Annie, they called her assaulted Molly's ears.

The old instinct to fight flared up. Molly turned. 'What? Your cheese? Why would I want your fucking cheese, you fat cow?'

Dark Annie's eyes narrowed. 'I seen you take the cheese off my plate when I was coming across the room. Don't fucking lie to me.'

And then it was fisticuffs, a flurry of slaps and a punch, scratching and grabbing the hair of the ugly cow and smacking her down. Molly knew the best way to attack was to attack first. It always came to fighting eventually and they all expected you to back off, not run at them. So hit them hard first.

The men pulled them apart. They enjoyed that; getting their hands all over the women for free.

'And you can fuck off too!' Molly snarled at John Dove making the filthy little burglar back off, fear in his eyes.

'I'll 'ave you, Molly McGlave,' Annie Chapman hissed, still being held back by two men and pretending she would have been at the fight again if they let her go, but she had a lump on her forehead where Molly had cracked her and blood on her lip.

Molly laughed theatrically, playing to her audience. 'You can try, you wee dwarf, but it'll take a better woman than you to beat me.'

Molly made a great play of taking her time to get ready, but as soon as she could with dignity she left the lodging house. She wandered the streets. She couldn't settle. Eventually, she got herself a gin and sat in the Blind Beggar for a while talking to whoever was in there. It was too early to be working, so she took it easy.

Everywhere was full of the gossip of Mary Nichol's murder and each account given was bloodier than the one before. Molly was shaken by it. She was surprised at herself. Nothing much touched her after these years on the street, but she remembered the noise of flapping wings and the smell of hot iron and the sheer unnaturalness of the man who had appeared from nowhere. She had decided she wasn't going to the police, but she had a strange need for the comfort of authority, so she went to church.

The Church of the English Martyrs lay a scant distance to the west of Whitechapel, near Tower Hill. They had built it after England allowed the emancipation of Catholics in 1829. She vaguely knew a priest there, Father Sheehan.

She found him and asked him to take her confession in the dim church that smelled of incense, shadowy and lit by clusters of brass sconced candles. Boys sang hymns in the dim wooden choir, as Molly settled herself in the confessional. Father Sheehan was from Donegal and Molly from Iniskeen in Monaghan, but they had a language in common. Molly's family had spoken nothing but Irish in her youth and it was in this language that father Sheehan heard her confession. She found her words running away with her. She gabbled, 'There was something unnatural about him, Father. That man. Devilish. He scared me to death. And then he killed Polly Nichol.'

The priest tried to calm her wildness. 'You don't have proof of that, my child. You can't be sure that the man you saw was the murderer. Better leave such suppositions to the English police.'

'But can a devil walk among men, father? The flapping of the wings and smell of iron?'

'To be sure, the devil does walk among men in disguise. And also sure, he was once an angel and was cast out of heaven.'

'And so would he have wings, father?'

'The common belief is that angels have wings, my child. But there is no authority for that, neither scriptural nor papal'

'So this could be the devil, father? This man I saw.'

The priest sighed heavily. 'I think it is best you forget this, Molly. But I want you to repent of your sinful life and give up the ways you have taken to. I want you to say ten Hail Marys and five Our Father's. If you can, you should give up the drink but most of all give up your sinful practices with men.'

'Yes, Father,' Molly said, though other than saying the prescribed prayers, she had no intention of doing anything else he suggested.

Father Sheehan said, 'You should leave this sinful city, Molly. It will be the end of you.'

'And where would I go, Father?'

He shrugged behind his screen. 'You could go back to Ireland, to your family.'

'Aye, I could go back to Ireland and starve.'

'Molly, I tell you, these streets will be your death.'

But Molly did not go back to Ireland; she went back to Whitechapel. The clouds cleared and the weather grew warm. It was September 1888, and Molly went back to work, and after she earned enough, she drank gin in the Frying Pan public house. But as she held her glass, everyone saw how her hand trembled. Though they put it down to the drink and did not know the black fears that ran through her.

THE FIRST WEEK IN SEPTEMBER, THE WEATHER WAS MIXED. THE entire summer had been a washout, cold with heavy rain, but there were days when it wasn't so bad. After her fight, Molly changed lodging houses to Thrawl Street. This was the lodging house that Mary 'Polly' Nichols had been living in just before she was murdered.

They were calling the murderer Jack the Ripper and claiming he had killed many others and that he would kill again. The streets were full of fear of him, but girls had to work if they wanted to eat and drink, even if all they drank was gin.

The talk of her death and various theories of the residents about who had killed her unsettled Molly's nerves, but at least that bitch Dark Annie wasn't there. Dark Annie was out to get her, and whenever Molly saw Annie Chapman, she avoided her.

After Polly Nichol's murder, Molly moved her pitch a bit, a little further west to Hanbury Street. She did all right there, getting money for doss, for gin and for the odd baked potato too. She spent the time she wasn't working sleeping at the doss house or in the pub: generally the Frying Pan, but sometimes the Blind Beggar or the Ten Bells.

She almost forgot about the wicked man with his flapping sound and his smell of iron until the Saturday. It was a bright morning, though Molly didn't see much of that, lying long in her bed. When she roused herself and got out, it was early afternoon. The weather was fair but threatening rain. First she had a drink. Molly set to work and got her first client around four. He was a docker who'd been on an early shift and then gone to the pub. It was a brief and rough coupling down an alley. 'You're all right, you,' he said. 'I'll be back.'

Molly smiled and thanked him and put the pennies in a linen pocket inside her blouse.

More came after. She took a break for gin and stayed in the Queen's Head until it was getting dark around nine p.m.

She felt safer away from Brook's Court and that end just off the Whitechapel Road, and Hanbury Street seemed to give her good trade. She stood waiting for work against the wall as raindrops pitter pattered and she had another client, then another and then more drink until she was half cut and then more clients and then a lull and a chat with some other girls, whose talk was still full of murders and the Ripper and death so Molly shivered and wandered away.

Then, late on, she saw Dark Annie and her heart fell. The fat bitch flounced up the Whitechapel Road with her missing teeth and Molly wondered how she got work. But then men were pigs, so what surprise was it they went with a sow?

Annie sneered. 'You bin avoiding me, you Fenian slut?' She wagged her finger, a foul smile on her face. 'You bin making yourself scarce, incha?'

Molly set herself up. She wouldn't show fear. 'So, I haven't been avoiding you, Annie. Why would I avoid a pathetic raddled aul' whore like yourself?'

'Cause you're scared I'll give you a kicking, and so I will, you bitch.'

'If you want to try, Annie, just make a start.'

Dark Annie hung back. 'Why don't you fuck off back to your own country and let an 'onest English woman get on with her own work? You fucking Tadhgs is always coming over here. It must be a right shit-hole back in Paddy land.'

'You English seem to like it well enough. If you didn't, you would have left us alone to have our own country.'

Annie laughed. 'Ere, word is you got a nice likkle patch up 'Anbury Street. Lot o' business up there, is there?'

Molly shrugged. 'It's as good as anywhere.'

'You better not be trying to keep an 'onest Englishwoman out. I fink I'll go and take a look.'

The last thing Molly wanted was Annie Chapman stealing her patch. She moved to block the way. For a minute she thought Annie would fight her there and then, but there was something in the other woman's eyes and a faint trembling of her lip that showed she thought better of it, at least until she was full of the courage more drink would give her.

Annie laughed. 'Changed me mind for now. But I tell ya, you foreigners don't got no rights 'ere. I'll work 'Anbury Street if I want to.'

'Off you go. Good on you.' Molly waved. 'I'll be seeing you then.'

Annie Chapman called over her shoulder. 'Not if I see you first, bitch.'

And with that Dark Annie turned and walked the other way.

THE RAIN FAIRED UP AND MOLLY FOUND HER WAY UP HANBURY Street. It wasn't so busy and it got quieter as the hours advanced. Molly heard the church clocks chiming the hours after midnight and as the air cooled, the fog gathered. River mist thickened by the coal of banked up fireplaces coiled and writhed like a grey snake, invading the streets and alleys. It got so thick she could hardly see anything. She knew it was dangerous to be out on a foggy night, and especially after the murder of Polly Nichols, everyone was on edge with fear of the Ripper. But still, as more and more of the girls dragged themselves to whatever roof they'd be stopping under that night, it meant less competition.

If Molly had a fault, it was that she liked money, though many others have that fault too. One more trick and there'd be a few pennies more in her pocket. She thought she'd just wait another quarter of an hour and if no knight in silver armour turned up, nor a scabby barrow boy with a couple of pennies to spend, then she'd make her way back to the doss house and bed.

It came through the air, faint at first. She heard it through the fog. The sound of beating wings, as if the trapped wings of an angel struggling to be free. And she smelled it again; the scent of hot iron; the scent she now recognised as the smell of blood.

Molly's heart rose into her throat. Her breathing grew tight. Her hands trembled ever so slightly. The sound and smell came for her, seeking her out. Molly hurried away towards people and pubs and the safety of the dosshouse.

But he appeared in front of her. He slipped through the wall like he was oil. He coalesced and formed and grew into the shape of a black cloaked man: top hat, opera cloak and face in shadow. She could hardly make him out through the fog, but she knew he was there in front of her. She darted left, within touching range of his fingers. She heard a moan in his throat. He radiated wickedness.

This was no man. Her first supposition was right: this was the Devil himself. No mortal could emerge through a wall. No mortal took shape like a nightmare from nothing on the foggy street. She was past him. If he reached after her and snatched at her, her she would scream. She hurried and she heard his steps come after her. She went faster and his pace quickened. She broke into a run, and he ran. And finally she went full pelt, her hands in her skirts so she did not trip.

She lost him in the fog. He was behind her still but out of sight. She ran through wreathes of obscuring mist; her ragged breath and the ricochet of her clumping boots sounding in the narrow street.

And then she saw Dark Annie emerge from the fog in front of her.

The other woman's face was fixed. 'What you running for, you stupid Irish bitch?'

Molly couldn't speak, she was so out of breath. She stopped, gasping. She had to warn Annie. She couldn't get her words out, she was so scared. Scared of the man who now lurked in the dark, stopping in the shadows, scenting an easier catch than Molly.

Dark Annie said, 'Don't be telling me I can't go up 'Anbury street, you slut. I go where I wants and no Paddy tells me I can't go as I choose in my own city.'

'Annie,' Molly said, finally getting enough air to form words. 'Don't go. There's a man there.'

Dark Annie laughed long and loud. 'Really?'

Molly reached out to grab Annie's arm to hold her back, but Annie was already walking off. She shook off Molly's grasp with a snarl and turned and struck Molly full in the face.

Molly reeled back and Annie said, 'Don't you fucking touch me ever again.' Annie had hit her hard, burst her lip, blood ran down her chin. Molly put her hand to her mouth, and as she did so, Annie walked off into the fog. From afar, she heard the woman's muffled call. ''Ello, there, sir. You looking for business?'

Terrified, she heard the indistinct voice of a man but couldn't catch his words. She could just see Annie and him in the gloomy street as shadows against shadows in the fog. Fear running through her, she called out, 'Annie! Don't go with him!'

But all Annie did was turn and yell, 'I thought I told you to fuck off. Now git gone!'

Molly stood trembling and bleeding as Dark Annie disappeared into the night with her mysterious stranger.

ANNIE CHAPMAN'S BODY WAS DISCOVERED A LITTLE BEFORE 6.00AM by John Davis, a dairyman who lived nearby.

Her murderer was never found.

❧ 2 ☙

THE HIGHGATE VAMPIRE

Dave "Smiler" Brown stepped inside from the warm summer night into the hall of a dilapidated, but once impressive three story house in Highgate. It wasn't quite a commune; it wasn't as organised as that. The inhabitants were colourful; there were various free spirits there and people kept coming and going, poets, dancers, writers, electricians and people who had completely dropped out of the rat race to take drugs in the upstairs rooms.

Smiler didn't take many drugs, just a bit of weed to relax him now and again. He avoided alcohol like the plague he saw what that had done to his dad. The odd tab of acid, but that was just recreation. Everyone in his circle did it. As for what he did for a living: well, he didn't really *do* anything. He tried some expressionist painting but he was crap at it. Couldn't play the guitar. Maybe he'd try the drums if one day he could get a drum kit. But something would turn up. Some talent would reveal itself. And it was only 1972 and he was on the dole. You could live like that then.

Smiler had been there at that big house for three months. Prior to that he was at another house in Hackney, but he preferred Highgate and he'd got in there because he'd known a bloke who told him about the squat. That bloke Michael was long gone now. He'd headed off to Marrakech with his girlfriend.

But it was all okay. Life was good. Smiler read comics a lot, mainly Thor, but inevitably some Superman. He had his own room, but there was a communal room with a gramophone that he also frequented. Right now Smiler relaxed with a rollie laced with herbal green, and bathed in the entertaining beats of *Led Zeppelin III*. The night was warm. He'd had a free meal from Denise and he had nothing in particular on his mind.

There were a couple of others in the room. They came and went. The only one who stayed and tried to make conversation was Leonard. Leonard was new to the squat and the killing thing about him was he was an albino. His hair was white as the Milky Bar Kid's, his face pale as talcum powder and his eyes as pink as the White Rabbit's. Even his eyelashes were white.

But that was miles and aeons away. Smiler shivered all over when the live version of *Smoke on the Water* pumped out of the record player.

Somebody spoke. 'Hello?'

Smiler was listening to the lyrics and singing along. 'We all came out to Montreux, on the Lake Geneva shoreline'

Smiler realised someone had changed the record without him noticing and wondered who did it. He didn't mind. He was very easygoing — live and let live. It had been Piper at the Gates of Dawn. He wasn't complaining. He never complained, that's why they called him Smiler!

'Hello?'

Someone was definitely calling him.

The voice came again. 'Hello, mate? Smiler, isn't it?'

The sound of his name finally summoned him back from a rolling, riding world of bass and guitar and drums. Smiler sailed in from a smooth world of mellow to the writhing smoke of the communal room where it smelled of cannabis and patchouli oil. His head was fuggy as he smiled at Leonard the Albino. 'Hey, man. What's happening?'

Leonard smiled with his pale pink lips; his pink eyes with surrounding white lashes like paintbrushes looked deep into Smiler's befuddled brown ones. Smiler's head felt smokey. 'Please ta meetcha, mate. I'm Smiler!'

'I'm Leonard. You been here long?'

'Here? Where's here, man? The planet?'

'Highgate.'

Smiler shrugged, took another toke of the reefer and said, 'I sailed in and one day I'm gonna sail out again.'

'Want to have some fun?' Lionel said, still looking calm and cold and white as a skinny washed out coffin worm brought to the surface by heavy rain.

Smiler grinned. 'Fun! Fun is my middle name, and my first name and my last name.'

Leonard laughed. 'I thought they called you Smiler?'

'Fun boy's always smiling,' Smiler said. He sat forward. 'Anyway, what's this about fun?'

'You heard of the Highgate Vampire?' Leonard said.

Smiler wasn't sure. He coughed. 'Yeah. I think.'

'It's in Highgate Cemetery.'

'I heard something.' Smiler took a deep drag, paused while it hit him and said, 'Guy in a hat? Drinks blood?'

'That's him.'

'Thought I heard something.'

Leonard said, 'Me and a friend are going there tonight.'

Smiler nodded. 'Lovely evening for it. The weather's been fantastic.'

'It'll be dark.'

'Sure. Essential for vampires, I guess.'

Leonard said, 'We're going to do an exorcism.'

Smiler blinked. 'Really? What for?'

'To get rid of the vampire.'

Smiler tilted his head. 'You want to get rid of it?'

'Of course, it kills people.'

'Really? Kills people? That's uncool. Shouldn't do that.'

'Do you want to come?'

'Me?'

'Yeah.'

'To kill a vampire?'

'To exorcise it. Drive it away.'

Smiler shrugged. 'Well...'

'My friend Elizabeth will be there.'

That piqued his interest. She sounded like a girl. Smiler liked girls. He was good with them. "Oh?' he said, Is she pretty?'

Leonard laughed. 'Stunning.'

Smiler rubbed his dreamy eyes. 'Yeah, okay then.'

NIGHT FELL. THE AIR WAS WARM AND SWEET AND SCENTED WITH night scented stocks and jasmine and honeysuckle from the rambling garden of the big house they were squatting in. Smiler got something to eat, looking out for Leonard but not seeing him and grateful for that, he went back to his room. Smiler was now level headed dope free and regretting saying he'd go wandering around in a graveyard in the dark. Still, there was this Elizabeth, supposedly pretty. But the question was, was she pretty enough to scare himself shitless? The hours ticked by on the gold wristwatch he'd inherited from his grandfather, the only classy item he owned, and Leonard's knock never came and Smiler breathed a sigh of relief.

He had the window open because the weather was so warm and he heard the Highgate clocks chime midnight. Time for another smoke. He felt mellow. This was his thing; he stayed up late and rose later, so midnight was early for Smiler.

Leonard opened Smiler's door without knocking, just as he was lighting up. 'You ready?'

Smiler froze. The albino's face was haunting in the electric light. It turned out Smiler found Leonard even weirder when he was sober. Smiler shrugged, palms up in a gesture of peace. 'Nah, I'm not sure, man. I got stuff to do.'

'Really?' Leonard sounded unconvinced

'Sure. I've got a book about meditation I was going to read. Some Indian guru wrote it.'

Leonard smiled sardonically. 'Or are you just chicken shit scared?'

Smiler jerked his thumb back to indicate himself with a wide-eyed look on his face that suggested Leonard's words were the dumbest thing ever said by anyone anywhere. 'Me? Scared?'

'Yeah, you.'

Smiler laughed. 'No, of course not. I've just got this book...'

'The book will wait. Come and meet Elizabeth. You'll like her. Unless you're a coward.'

That gave Smiler pause. Though he was a free spirit and all of that and didn't mind being called dirty and work-shy, because the people who said that were all slaves to the rat race, but being thought a coward didn't sit easy with him. 'But Leonard...'

'Come on. Elizabeth will meet us there.'

Smiler exhaled deeply. Without much enthusiasm, he followed Leonard down the stairs and out the front door and along the garden path between rose bushes run wild then out through a wrought-iron gateway twined with honeysuckle and ivy, until they emerged onto the street.

A short walk from the squat, and they were at the top of Swain's Lane. This steep, narrow lane led to the graveyard, flanked by high walls like a sunken ceremonial route to hell.

Smiler threw his head back. It was such a lovely night. The moon was up, big and yellow and she smiled down on them, casting ink black shadows where she didn't reach and washes of white ivory where she did. Black and white, black and white, like a chessboard, they walked, amid scents of damp willows, dreaming oaks, and resinous yews.

Smiler knew, because he was not an ignorant man, that Highgate Cemetery was built in the 1830s and filled with overdone funeral monuments which had gone to rot and ruin since the company ran out of money in the 1960s. No one officially entered the cemetery now and the tombs and pathways were overgrown and home to foxes and owls, to night flitting bats and apparently to vampires.

'We'll go in the North Gate,' Leonard said. 'It's quieter. We'll have to climb over the gate though.'

'Where's your girlfriend?' Smiler said.

'She's not my girlfriend. Just a friend, and she said she'd meet us here.'

It was a lovely night, but the thought of breaking into a graveyard unnerved Smiler a little. He said, 'No sign of her yet. Want to wait here?'

'No, let's just go in. She can meet up with us in there.'

'Oh,' Smiler said, scratching the back of one hand with the other. 'I'd rather wait for her out here.'

Leonard's pallid face gleamed sweaty and white in the pellucid moonlight. 'Come on, you shithouse.'

And with that, Leonard mounted the gate and vaulted the top of the chained up gateway. Smiler heard a soft thump as Leonard landed in the piled up leaf mulch on the other side. Smiler swallowed hard. On reflection, he really didn't want to be doing this.

'Come on!' Leonard hissed impatiently out of sight.

He could slink back to the squat, but then Leonard would tell everyone he was yellow. Smiler sighed. He was dying for a smoke and he didn't have any.

'Come on. Elizabeth's waiting,' Leonard hissed.

Smiler shrugged. Maybe he would get something out of this. They might have some cigarettes. Then there was the so far unseen Elizabeth. That cheered him up. Girls liked him, they said he was vulnerable and charming. He played up to that all the time with good results.

Resignedly, he climbed and dropped into the darkness behind the padlocked gate. It was Bible black here under the cover of confused and interlocking trees. The undergrowth grew thick and bindweed and ivy fingers entwined above his head, blocking out the creamy moon. His feet sank in the damp mulch. The smell of woodlands assailed his nostrils. He couldn't see Leonard.

'Here,' the albino whispered. 'I'm here.'

Smiler couldn't make out much in the gloom, but the sound came from further up the path.

As he set off, an owl called further into the cemetery, like a guard announcing their arrival.

Smiler hurried on after Leonard. Leonard seemed to know where he was going. They walked fast along trails that ran between overdone Victorian tombs. Sometimes Leonard would hesitate, as if unsure, and then grunt and go on. Smiler had to hurry to catch up.

Then they came to a crossroads. The trees didn't reach here and the white moon sailed high overhead. For the first time, since they entered Highgate Cemetery, Smiler could see Leonard's strange pale face. For the first time, now he was standing still, breathing lightly, he realised how scared he was.

He bit his lip. What the hell was he doing in the middle of Highgate Cemetery at midnight with some bloke he didn't know?

Smiler's heart thumped gently in his chest. His palms were sweaty. 'What now?' he said.

'We wait.'

'Wait? For what?'

'For me.' A woman's voice whispered from the shadows behind. Startled, Smiler spun round. A young woman, maybe twenty-five, stepped out of the trees. She wore the shadows like a cloak and was unutterably beautiful. Her hair was black, and her face was moon pale and tinged with some of the phosphorescence of that heavenly body. Her lips were crimson and her eyes were like blue pools beneath her black eyebrows. She was stunning, slim with thrusting bosoms and a narrow waist that flared to full hips under her taffeta dress.

'Meet Elizabeth,' Leonard said, with a mock bow. At least Smiler thought it was a mock bow, but this girl could in fact be royalty from the air of authority and command that exuded from her.

'Hi, I'm Smiler,' he said.

Elizabeth put out her gloved hand. She wore a golden ring with a red stone set in it on her ring finger over the glove. Without knowing why he did it, he bent and kissed her ring.

She laughed, a sweet, tinkling sound that made his spine tingle and a sweetness like cream soda rose up into his solar plexus.

'Pleased to meet you, Smiler.'

'Me you too, Elizabeth.'

Leonard grinned. 'See? I told you, you'd like her. Everyone does.'

Elizabeth laughed again. 'Leonard is such a charmer. But not everyone likes me. Far from it.'

'Let's go on,' Leonard said.

They set off at a pace, Leonard leading, Smiler walking side by side with Elizabeth behind. Smiler ran his hand through his hair trying to smooth it. 'So, we're doing a vampire hunt,' he said.

'An exorcism,' Leonard called back.

'Sure.' He turned to the young beauty beside him. 'Hey, do you believe in vampires, Elizabeth?'

'Oh yes, I'm sure they exist.'

'But here? In Highgate? In London?'

'Why not?' Elizabeth said. Even her velvety voice was seductive.

'There are lots of reports,' Leonard called back.

Smiler ignored him. He was talking to Elizabeth. 'Really though? A tall man in a top hat?'

She shrugged in the moonlight. 'I don't know about that.'

Smiler couldn't believe that anyone so beautiful would believe this crap. With her there beside him, it was important he didn't show the sizzle of anxiety that was running through him from being here in the graveyard.

Smiler was about to suggest to Elizabeth that maybe they could meet up for a coffee or a smoke the next day when Leonard stopped. 'Here,' he said.

Smiler hadn't been paying attention to where they were. He turned from Elizabeth and saw massive ornate stonework in front of him. This wasn't a single tomb, it was a mausoleum. And it wasn't a mausoleum for a single family but some Victorian architect's idea of ancient Egypt.

A massive stone rampart stood in front of them. Weeds and trees grew from the top but the architecture looked Ancient Egyptian, like the temple at Luxor that he had seen in his dad's National Geographic. A deep shadow haunted gate led within. Once there had been a wooden huge double door, but that now hung broken on one side, and the other half-door off its hinges and pushed open into the tunnel.

'Behold the Circle of Lebanon,' Leonard said with a flourish.

Smiler's mouth was dry. 'We're going in there?' he said. He heard the quaver in his voice and tried to disguise it, but Elizabeth heard it anyway and laughed softly. She said, 'You're not scared are you, Smiler?'

He blushed. 'Of course not. It's just it's maybe not safe.'

It was Leonard's turn to laugh. 'No, it's not safe. That's why we're going.'

Smiler cleared his throat. 'To do this exorcism?'

'Yes,' Elizabeth said.

'Thing is, I don't believe in vampires,' Smiler said.

Elizabeth stroked his arm. 'Then there's nothing to worry about.'

'What if the place falls on us? It looks old and crumbly.'

'It won't. We've been there before,' Leonard said.

Smiler's mouth went dry and his heart beat faster. He struggled to get his words out, then said, 'I'm okay guys. I think I'm going to miss this.'

Elizabeth laughed again.

'Come on, Smiler.' Leonard coaxed him. 'You wouldn't want your friends at the squat thinking you'd chickened out.'

Smiler frowned. No he wouldn't. There was something strange about this. They were so insistent that he go. It didn't make sense. Why did they care if he went or not? But then it occurred to him they were maybe going to murder him. Maybe they were a couple who got weird sexual kicks out of murdering strangers. He stepped back, 'No.'

'Come on!' Leonard said, getting angry. 'Don't waste my time, Smiler. You said you'd come. The tomb's just here. Just inside and to the right.'

'That's right,' Elizabeth said. 'Just inside the Circle. Just within the gate.'

'No, sorry, I'm leaving.'

'You won't find your way out on your own,' Leonard said.

Smiler's heart was going wild now with a pitter patter of palpitations like butterfly wings. He felt sweat prickle his back. He stepped back again. It was true. He'd never find his way out. But at least he wouldn't be here. He stepped back again. He half turned. He thought of running.

Then Elizabeth said, 'Let him go. You go with him. Show him the way out.'

He heard the anger in Leonard's voice behind. 'If you're sure.'

Elizabeth nodded. 'Maybe you'll come back tomorrow?' she said to Smiler.

He swallowed hard. 'Sure. I just wasn't in the mood tonight.'

'Of course.' She leaned up and kissed him on the cheek. Her lips were full and soft and chill.

'I'll take him to the North Gate,' Leonard said.

'I'll wait for you here until you come back,' Elizabeth said. 'Then we'll do our ceremony.'

SMILER MANAGED TO AVOID LEONARD THE NEXT TWO DAYS. IT WAS Friday when he bumped into him in the kitchen. He still looked weird.

'Hey, man,' Leonard said. 'Had an attack of the nerves the other night, eh?'

'No,' Smiler said as he buttered some half-burned toast. He had some baked beans on the gas ring, bubbling away nicely. 'Just wasn't my thing.'

'Funny, I thought you were into it.'

'No.' Smiler went to pour the beans on the now buttered toast and sit down at the cluttered table. There was some pepper somewhere. He liked pepper on his baked beans.

'Elizabeth liked you.'

Smiler sat back. 'She did?'

'Yeah.'

Smiler remembered that he liked her too. He remembered the soft brush of her lips on his cheek.

He grinned. 'She was pretty cool.'

'She knows. She knows you like her too."

'Ah' Smiler blushed. He hated being obvious, though he knew he probably often was.

'We're going again tonight,' Leonard said.

Smiler went back to eating, expertly slicing a strip of beans and toast.

Leonard continued. 'Elizabeth wondered if you would come along.'

Smiler shook his head. 'Not sure.'

'She said if we go earlier, we can maybe go round her place after and have a drink and a smoke.'

Smiler looked up now. 'She lives in Highgate?'

'Yeah. Not far. She's got wine she said.'

Smiler remembered how pretty she was. 'How long does this exorcism thing take?'

Leonard shrugged. 'Not so long. She just likes the occult and things. I just do it for her.'

Smiler laughed. 'You ever...?'

Leonard shook his head. 'Oh, no. I'm not her type.'

Smiler chewed the soggy toast and swallowed. 'Okay. I'll come along. It's not my thing, but if we're going back to hers...'

Leonard said. 'I would come back with you, but I've got another date, so I can't stay.'

Smiler mused. 'So just me and her?'

'Apparently.' Leonard was grinning now. He winked.

It was only half ten when they scaled the graveyard gate and dropped onto the soft earth of the other side. Smiler hissed. 'Where are we meeting Elizabeth?'

'I'm here,' said a velvety voice just behind his shoulder. 'I was waiting for you.'

'Elizabeth!' Smiler said. He couldn't help living up to his name, though he could hardly see her in the gloom, but he recognised her voice. She reached over and ran her hand up and down his bicep. 'Let's go,' she said.

'Then we're going for a drink?'

'Sure.'

'Leonard can't come,' Smiler said.'He says.'

'So he told me. All the more for us then.'

'I smoke more than I drink,'

She smiled in the shadows. 'Wine is my poison; the redder the better.'

Smiler thought of the warmth of the night. 'You don't need to chill red wine either, but you've probably got a fridge.'

'No,' she said. 'I like it warm.'

They stood again before the great decayed entrance to the Circle of Lebanon. The moon tonight cast no light, instead she hid her face behind clouds as if afraid of witnessing what was about to happen. The monuments to the dead were wreathed in shadow and weeds.

Something moved in the tangled briars to their left. Smiler jumped despite himself. Leonard laughed.

Elizabeth said, 'Probably a fox. Don't worry.'

'Or a rat,' Leonard said.

'A rat?' Smiler was alarmed now. He didn't like rats.

'Let's go into the Circle of Lebanon,' Elizabeth said, taking Smiler's hand. He felt her gloved fingers twine through his. He had a lump of anxiety in his throat as she pulled him forward into the tunnel that led to the inner circle. It was unlikely they were really going to murder him. He saw the doors of tombs on each side as they came to the crescent and the way split going left and going right.

Elizabeth led him right.

'Is it far?' he asked. His voice didn't sound right. He hoped she didn't notice.

'Not far,' she said.

They walked on, stepping over dead branches and fallen masonry. Mice scuttled away underfoot and bats flitted in the air above. Smiler glanced up. Even in the darkness of the moonless night, he could see they were in a deep channel of masonry. Tombs seemed piled up on top of each other. There were sepulchre doors on both sides, some gaping open.

He was afraid.

Still Elizabeth held his hand and tugged him on. Leonard went in front of them.

'Far still?' he asked.

'Not far,' said Elizabeth.

A few more careful paces, stepping over fallen bricks and pieces of rotten wood then Leonard stopped. 'Here,' he said.

'Yes,' Elizabeth said. 'This is it.'

Smiler's voice shook. 'Will it take long, it's just that...'

She stroked his arm, calming him like he was a young bull going to the abattoir. 'It won't take long,' she said soothingly.

'And then we'll go for a drink?' he asked her, his voice stammering.

She nodded, leaning in, kissing him with her plump, soft lips on his cheek.

He put his hand up to where her lips had touched his skin. He felt an imprint of ice where there should be warmth.

Elizabeth whispered, 'Then we will drink, yes.'

Smiler looked at her sapphire blue eyes, that seemed almost to give off their own light, and her lips painted incarnadine. She was close. Close enough to kiss. Her breath should be warm against his skin, a gentle sigh of life, but Smiler felt no breath.

Leonard opened the door of the tomb then stood.

The sense of apprehension grew in Smiler's breast. Leonard was waiting for something.

'Light the candles,' Elizabeth said.

Smiler and she waited outside while Leonard went into the tomb.

Smiler heard the scrape and flare of a match and saw a fluttering flame kindle inside the cold silent sepulchre. He said, 'I'm not sure about this.'

Elizabeth whispered into his ear. 'Don't worry, my love.'

She was so sensual. So soft. So seductive. He felt her whispers caress him. She stroked his face with her satin fingers.

'Ready,' Leonard called from inside the tomb.

Elizabeth pulled him forward. He half-resisted, then gave in. His pulse pounded. His throat tightened. He couldn't swallow. He fought to control his anxiety. He mustn't show his fear. Elizabeth wouldn't hurt him. She was so close, so close to him now. He felt her cold bones against him.

They stepped to the door. Four red candles flickered in the breeze and shadows danced around the decayed tomb. In all the corners the darkness frolicked and fluttered as if awaiting a celebration.

He could hardly get his words out. He tried to sound normal. 'This is an exorcism?'

They ignored him.

Leonard looked at Elizabeth. Something was wrong. Smiler looked at her beseechingly. She only smiled.

He saw in the tomb there was a single shelf and on that shelf was a coffin. The coffin looked old. The top of the coffin was removed but there was no body in it.

'I don't get it,' Smiler said, relief flooding over him. He almost laughed. 'Where's the vampire?'

Elizabeth giggled, putting her hand to her mouth to stifle it. Smiler looked at her quizzically then back at the coffin. There was a small tarnished brass nameplate screwed into the old varnished wood. Smiler peered at it. He couldn't read it from where he stood, and it seemed suddenly important that he read it. He stepped forward. They didn't prevent him. Smiler traced the words of the engraving with the tips of his fingers to read it better.

It said:

Here lie the remains of Elizabeth Bell: Cursed in Life: Cursed in Death. May the Lord have mercy should she rise again.

Smiler began to tremble. 'I don't like this,' he said. He was sweating. He was shaking. He was unbearably cold. 'Can we go to yours now, Elizabeth?' he said.

Elizabeth's crimson lips were half open. Her blue eyes glittered with wicked luminescence. Her teeth were long and white and sharp. Her face was pale as new fallen snow. 'Oh, Smiler,' she said. 'We already have.'

❦ 3 ❦

NOISES FROM THE ATTIC

I moved into the house towards the end of the year when the nights darkened and chilly winds blew from Camden all the way to Wapping. I liked the location — right by the river — close to that famous pub *The Prospect of Whitby* that stands on the bank of the River Thames. They say the pub was built in 1520, a haunt of pirates, whores and judges.

I worked at a hospital not too far away. I liked the olde worldie atmosphere of the Prospect and I used to drink there even before I moved into that house. Funny how I came across the house by chance. I wish I hadn't now.

Julie was my landlady. I met her and her boyfriend James in the Prospect. She worked at the same hospital I did. She pitched the rent ridiculously low, far below market value. So low, I thought maybe she fancied me. But it wasn't that. I wish it was really.

I don't know what to say about the house. Did I like it? It had character; it was interesting. It was historic even, and without doubt I was lucky to be living there in such a fantastic location at such a low rent, but did I like it? No, not at all. Not for a minute.

The house was old. I don't know if it was as old as the *Prospect of Whitby,* but it was at least 18th Century, if not earlier. It too looked over the lazy, dirty Thames as the cold, brown water flowed endlessly to the sea. Funnily enough, though I didn't like the house, I enjoyed standing in the small backyard, looking out onto the misty Thames on those cold, slow days of winter.

To cap the place's charms, we weren't far from Execution Dock, where they chained pirates at low water and left them to drown as the tide came in. I thought one time, maybe the entire thing about the house was something to do with that. But it wasn't.

The house belonged to Julie's father. She told me it had been in the family for generations, but her dad lived elsewhere - out in the leafy suburbs with his new, young wife. Maybe he didn't like the house either.

But the place was handy for me and the rent was very reasonable, as I said.

My bedroom was up on the top floor, facing the street, so no river view, though I could of course go into the backyard with a cup of coffee and gaze at boats.

There were plenty of other rooms in the house — it was big — but their doors were mostly locked. The ones I could see into were full of clutter - mouldy old books, piles of car magazines from 1972, and her dad's old model railway that no longer worked. Downstairs was the living room with its sofas, its TV, its wooden floor and big Persian rugs. There was a dining room and an old-fashioned kitchen that badly needed a refit.

When did it all start? The tapping was the first thing. It began in mid-October. I used to lie on my bed looking at the ceiling, wondering what the hell was making the noise. It was rhythmic, but not always the same rhythm. Just a light tapping. Light mostly, but sometimes so loud it would wake me up. And sometimes it went crazy and the rhythm went off, beating like a pumped up heart about to die. I tried to see if the noise coincided with heavy rain, in case it was water dripping, as if maybe the rain was getting into the roof space and tap tap tapping down just above my head. Somehow I convinced myself it was. That explanation put my mind at rest for a while.

My landlady, Julie, spent her time at her new boyfriend Brian's place. The old boyfriend James had been a journalist. I sort of got on with him. Brian was a big rugby playing jock type. He was OK with me, but we had little to talk about. He had no interest in cardiology and I very little in rugby. But Julie appeared infatuated with him; she would stand there, with her arms draped round him as he talked about whatever pointless shit was on his very tiny mind and she smiled and looked up in awe.

I said to her one morning, "What the hell is that dripping that I hear from the attic?"

I swear she went white. "Dripping?" she said.

I couldn't get over her body language. She looked really freaked out. It was an everyday question for her to look so spooked about. I said, "Yeah, the tapping noise. It's like water has got in. You want to get someone up there to check out the roof."

"There is no attic," she said in a definite tone of voice.

"In an enormous house as old as this? No attic?" It seemed strange, but I couldn't believe it was something anyone would lie about.

She shook her head. "No attic. Nothing like that. But maybe there is rain getting in somewhere. I'll ask my dad to get it checked out.' She frowned. 'Does it bother you?"

"Well, not mostly. Sometimes it's loud. It comes and goes, you know."

"I'll ask Dad to get it seen to. Don't worry."

I shrugged. "I'm not worried. It's your house."

Then she changed the subject and asked me how work was.

THE NOISE WENT AWAY FOR ABOUT A WEEK, SO I HAD SOME refreshing baby sleep. Work was busy. There were spending cuts and we lost some staff; the rest of us just had to fill in. So when I went home after my shifts on the ward, I slept deeply.

One night, midweek. I woke and knew something was wrong. It was about two in the morning and a loud scraping noise exactly like something being dragged across floorboards came from the space above my room. That sure as hell wasn't rain. I lay there with my heart racing. There was silence for about five minutes. I kidded myself I'd maybe dreamed it, and I rolled over to try to sleep when I heard scratching again. Then I tried to convince myself that maybe birds had got in under the roof. That would account for the scratching, but not that awful dragging noise.

The scratching came again the next night. It alternated with the tapping noise. It happened the night after that too. It unnerved me, and I took to staying at friends' houses instead of coming home to sleep. To tell the truth, more than once I deliberately drank myself into oblivion so I could stay somewhere far away from that house in Wapping. I thought about moving out — finding somewhere more conducive, but the rent was too good. The location was too good. I told myself the entire thing about the noises was just my imagination, and it was irrational to let it get on top of me like it was.

I came back more, slept in my own bedroom, told myself it had all been because of stress.

THEN ONE NIGHT JULIE AND BIG BRIAN WERE AT HOME. WE cracked open a bottle of wine downstairs while we watched some glitzy big budget talent show on TV. Work had gone well; I was in an excellent mood. I was getting on with Brian. He said, "Why don't we go to the Prospect?"

It seemed a wonderful idea. The pub wasn't far away and so even though it was raining and the winter night still cold and cloudy; we walked through the narrow streets of Wapping with their tasteful repro Victorian street lamps to the Prospect of Whitby. Once inside, Brian bought me a drink, "You're not a bad guy for a nurse," he said.

'Thanks, I think.'

He laughed and sank half his pint in one gulp. Two drinks in, I found my courage. "Hey," I said to Julie. "What's with that scratching?"

She pretended she didn't know what I was talking about.

I said. "You must have noticed it. You've lived in that house all your life."

"I was away at school and we mostly lived in Surrey..." she protested.

"Even so. You must have heard the scratching."

"No," she said, clearly wanting to end this conversation. There was something about her tone of voice that made me suspicious. I still couldn't see what motivation she'd have to lie about some seagulls getting under the roof. The rest of the time in the pub, she avoided my gaze. Brian had finished his beer. "Beer good!" he said. "Let's get another!"

And so we got another and the conversation moved on and for nearly a week things were okay.

On that Thursday, Julie was in. I was in my room. She was in hers, studying for an exam she had the next day — part of her continuing professional development. I was reading a science fiction novel. I was light years away on a huge gas giant planet when the scratching came. But much louder.

I jumped off my bed and stood in the middle of the room. My heart hammered and my throat tightened. Then the noise came again. This time I was sure it was an animal. Something big - almost man sized. I flung my door open and half ran down the upstairs corridor to Julie's room. I banged on the door.

She opened the door. "What?" She seemed pissed off that I'd disturbed her.

"That!" I said. I could still hear it. It was centred above my room.

"What?" she said again.

"That noise."

"I can't hear any noise."

I was incredulous. "You're joking, right? That awful scratching sound. What the hell is up there?"

"Up where?"

"There must be an attic."

"I told you. The house has no attic."

"Come to my room. You can hear it."

Reluctantly, she followed me. We stood in my room. Now there was nothing - not a sound; as if it was conspiring with her. She shrugged. "I think you're imagining it."

"I'm not," I said. We waited. Still nothing. I felt deflated — foolish. We waited a bit longer. She turned and said, "I need to get back to studying."

And then the noise came again — a scrabbling sound, like something with claws.

She stopped, but didn't turn to face me.

I said, "See, that's not rain. It's something."

She still didn't turn round.

"Julie," I said, "Come on. You can surely hear that."

Her silence was annoying me. The scratching came again — a frantic scrabbling as if something was trying to dig its way through the ceiling into my room.

"Say something," I said. "What is that?"

A dark suspicion formed in my mind that she knew exactly what it was. I said, "I can't sleep with that noise. What is it? Some kind of secret pet or something?"

"I've got to get back to my studying," she said.

"But you can't leave me with that noise."

"It'll stop soon. It always does."

So she did know. She walked out of my room without looking back. I followed her. She went into her room and turned round, the door handle in her hand ready to close it in my face. I stood there and said, "What's really going on?"

She shook her head and said vehemently, "Nothing."

She was standing at the door of her room and I looked past her. There was a hatch in the ceiling. Like the door to an attic.

The next day Julie was gone early and I missed her at breakfast time. I watched morning TV as I wasn't due in at work until the late shift began at 2pm. I didn't go outside, but I stayed downstairs. The bottom of the house seemed okay. It was at the top of the house that I felt uneasy.

Then I decided I was going to find out what was really going on in that house.

I went upstairs. I knocked on Julie's door just to make sure I hadn't got it wrong and she was in there asleep. There was no answer. I waited. I knocked again. And then, after three minutes of silent hesitation, I pushed the door open. It was a messy girl's room. The bed was unmade. Her pyjamas lay around; the top on the bed, the bottoms on the floor. Two nursing textbooks also lay on the floor next to a pad filled with notes about blood results. It was all so normal.

Then I looked up at that hatch in the ceiling. It had been painted white. It looked fixed. I wondered when it had been opened last. I got her chair from the dressing table and I moved it so I could stand right under the hatch. I got up on it and reached up, prodding with my fingers. The door into the attic didn't give but as I looked closer, I could see that the edges of the oblong door up into that space had odd scratch marks on them, as if something with very long nails had opened it and scratched away the paint. I couldn't budge it.

And then for two nights nothing happened. No scratching. The third night I stayed at a friend's house in Crouch End. The fourth night I went back. Brian was in. We cracked a bottle of wine and watched the football: England v. Macedonia. Macedonia won.

"It's only got a population of about a thousand. How can they fucking win?" asked Brian.

"Dunno, mate. Let me refresh your glass."

Then we watched the IT Crowd. I said, "Brian, did Julie ever speak to you about the attic?"

He shook his head. "Nope. Is there an attic?"

"You've been in her room?"

He looked at me as if I was stupid. "I'm her boyfriend. So yes."

"Have you noticed the door in the ceiling?"

He shook his head again. "No. Is there one?"

I nodded. "Yes."

"Oh, you mean that hatch thing?"

"Yeah. That."

He shrugged. "It's just a hatch. I don't think it opens."

"But where's it lead to?"

"The Attic?"

He didn't look bothered.

"Have you heard the scratching?"

"Sure. Thought it was birds."

"So did I."

He sipped his beer. "It's not birds?"

"I don't think so."

"So what's scratching?"

"I don't know." I paused. "Should we go and look?"

He laughed. "Look in the attic?"

"I just want to know what's in there."

"You're crazy."

"But do you want to look?"

"Julie would go mental. She doesn't like me in her room if she's not there. Anyway, she's back soon. Should be home about eleven."

"She won't let us look. I think she's hiding something." The wine had made me a bit too open. He looked at me long and hard. Then he said, "Macedonia, eh? Who the fuck would have thought they'd have beat us? It's a fucking disgrace."

Julie came home and they started canoodling so I went to bed. And then, in the depths of the night, I heard it again. The house was quiet. It was long after they'd gone to bed. It must about been about three a.m. I thought whatever it was - it was trying to scrape its way through the floor and come and get me.

Then Brian stopped coming. She never said they'd finished. I just never saw him again.

My plan was that I'd wait until Julie was out and I'd go look in the attic for myself. But I needed equipment. I went to a hardware store and got a flashlight and a crowbar in case I needed to prise the hatch open. Until the time came, I kept all my gear in a sports bag at work. The night I decided to do it, I was on a late shift and I got back about half ten. I let myself into the house with my key. The downstairs was in darkness. I flicked the light on and began to make my way upstairs. I was scared, but I told myself not to be.

What could be in the attic? I thought what I would find would be some birds. I was shaking. I told myself if it was birds they would be frightened of me, not the other way round. But I didn't think it was birds.

I went up the stairs. I could feel my heart banging. I'd just pull the chair until it was under the hatch; open it and drag myself up, shine the flashlight around and that would be that.

But I couldn't do it. I hesitated outside the door and the moment I hesitated my courage disappeared. I told myself I'd not done it because I didn't need to, but it was really because I feared what was in the attic.

I went to bed. I slept. Much later, the scratching woke me. It was middle of the night and the room was cold.

The scratching kept on. I leaned over to switch on the angle-poise lamp by my bed. I clicked the switch, but nothing happened. Tentatively, I got up out of bed. I switched on the room light by the wall. No light, just an empty click. There must be a power outage.

I opened the door. And then I stopped.

Above me the scratching had gone silent, but out in the corridor I heard a breathing — a ragged breathing. And then I got the strangest idea, as if something had dropped from the attic and come into the house.

Something had come from the attic and was now standing there in the corridor.

There was no lock on my door. I closed it as quietly as I could, hoping that the thing with its tortured breath would not hear. And I held the door handle, shaking with fear. It had been in the attic. Now it was walking the house.

I opened the door half an inch and put my eye to the crack in the door.

Through the crack, I saw a face. Something watched me, its face pressed against the crack in the door. Its breath in my cheeks. Its blind, white, boiled eyes looking into mine.

I jumped back. I tripped and fell on my back. As I scrabbled to get up, the door slowly opened.

It was tall and covered in flesh that hung in ribbons. Teeth filled its face. Its hair hung long and dirty and it stunk of old meat. The thing, taller than a man, wheezed as it entered my room. Its long arms dragged on the floorboards; its dirty nails clattered as it shuffled in.

In the half light from the window, I saw its mouth open and it sniffed for me. Its white eyes were blind; it hunted by scent. The thing that lived in the attic had come down for me.

Panic ran through me like electricity. But fear gave me strength and quickness. I jumped and rolled. I went to push past it. It sensed me. It turned and grabbed. Its fingers gripped my forearm, cold and greasy. I dragged myself away. I pulled free. The stink of it filled my nostrils like something dead by the roadside.

And there was Julie at the door of her room. She stood there fully dressed. I said, 'Julie, you must come. That thing...'

'The thing from the attic,' she said. She was smiling.

It turned in my room, smelling me. It walked slowly towards me down the corridor.

I couldn't figure out why she was smiling. 'Julie, we've got to get out of here.'

She grinned and grabbed my arm, holding me tight.

I struggled to free myself as the thing from the attic shuffled towards me. Julie's grip held me so I couldn't get away from it.

She wanted it to have me. 'You've lived longer than most of the men in my life. Time's up now.'

'Let me go!' I begged.

But she said, 'If you go, what will my monster eat?'

It was close now. Only feet away. I recoiled from its stink. The monster raised its long hands with its filthy fingers. Its mouth full of teeth opened, snapping for me.

With a burst of terrified strength, I yanked myself from Julie's grasp and ran, almost falling down the stairs.

I got to the front door. But it was locked.

The thing from the attic descended the stairs after me. Julie stood behind it with the door key. She wagged her finger. 'Didn't you think I'd think of that?'

And then I remembered the kitchen. I ran as the thing came down the stairs, now within feet. I only hoped Julie had forgotten to lock the kitchen door. I got to it, panicked going for the handle, finally, getting a grip on it, turned the metal handle, hand shaking, and shoved it half expecting the door to be locked and the thing to catch me, but the door came open and I emerged onto the balcony. The frigid London air hit me. The Thames was before me, the thing pushed through the door out onto the balcony behind snapping and snatching. I looked at the river water. There was no contest.

I jumped in and nearly drowned. I swam, and swam pulled by the river until I came to shore a hundred yards to the seaward side, carried by the current and frozen by the cold. But I got out of the river dripping wet. I got out and I never went back to Wapping. I left all my things there and never called to collect them. I count myself lucky.

If you ever meet a girl called Julie, and get the offer of a house, and then she casually mentions a rent that seems too good to be true, walk on by.

4

A DOCTOR CALLS

Once Soho was fashionable. Now it's a melting pot of disease, poverty and vice, but also of colour and diversity and life. From my words, you understand that I am still very attached to the area where I have lived most of my life. My name is Alexander Graham, a Scot, trained at Edinburgh, but in London since I qualified. By profession, I am a physician.

Until the thing I am about to recount occurred, I saw myself completely as a man of science, treating infections with bromide and iodine, treating syphilis with mercury, and though these remedies may sound quaint, in my practice they were mainstay. I could say we knew no better, but the truth was we had no alternatives, so these tinctures were a counsel of desperation for illnesses we could not cure.

I have devoted my life to the study of disease, given money to research, participated in research, even on some occasions been a subject of research with colleagues, but still disease took the lives of so many around us. Yet we went on, secure in our conviction that more research would bring results to alleviate the suffering of our patients.

As I alluded initially, the rich once lived in Soho, but after the Earl of Scarborough developed Mayfair, the fashionable folk spread west and Soho filled in their wake with French Huguenot refugees. That was in the 18th Century, and some remain of those, but since that time we have Italians, Lascars, Malays and Chinese. As I wander the busy narrow streets about my business, I admit I enjoy the babble of languages and the smells of different cuisines. Somehow it gives heart to a district in daytime, where strange things walk at night on the darkened streets. It is as if life surges onto the street as the sun rises, but retreats behind locked doors when dusk returns.

Few of the people I serve have money, but some others are still rich, so I split my time between treating patients who can pay and whose cash subsidises the poor whom I visit for the good of both their health and my soul. These pay me as best they can, with food, with charms, with prayers but mostly only with their thanks, and that is enough.

It was a winter's evening when Reverend Appleby summoned me to his house, a night when low-lying fog shrouded the Soho streets. I strolled briskly as misty fingers invaded Soho Square and yellow vapours filled side roads and alleys. Gas lamps burned with vague halos and the laughter of prostitutes echoed down narrow closes as the mist seethed all round in seductive tendrils, concealing all manner of crime and vice.

I HAD BEEN TO SEE A CHINESE MAN WHO'D CUT HIS ARM AT WORK and it had become infected. He bore the pain well as I applied my astringent chemicals. I told him that as he was strong and relatively young he should survive his wound. That call was off Peter Street. My next and last call of the evening was to the aforementioned Reverend Appleby. I had not met him before, as a colleague who had since retired had previously treated him. I had received his card in the early evening, and though he was a paying customer, my prior obligation to the Chinese labourer called upon my sense of Hippocratic duty. That done, now it was his turn to be seen.

He was a William Appleby, apparently respectable and relatively prosperous. He was still vicar at St Anne's church, though I understood he had a curate increasingly do most of the work for him while he retired to libraries to work on some unknown literary project of his own. This gossip I had from my clerk, though with few further details. From symptoms described on the card, I suspected this was another case of pneumonia; an exceedingly common disease made worse by the perennial London fog that even now cloaked my way and made my footsteps ring unnaturally loud, their echo reverberating from sooty brick walls.

As I walked, I passed St Anne's churchyard and knew the vicarage lay just past that. I marched, collar up against the damp, past the church. The church sat well back from the road; the tombstones decayed and corroded, standing skew like a field of stone teeth before it.

In daylight, St Anne's church was fine enough, but by night the place always made me uneasy. At first I thought my fear came from the idea of low fellows in the churchyard, but I told myself what would even they be doing out in such weather as this?

As I walked, I heard a noise. It was not like a noise I had ever heard before. I stopped to listen, as an unnatural dread seeped into me. It was an indistinct whispering sound, almost like a breeze through dry leaves, but louder than that, with sounds that rose repeating and insinuating as if words in a strange tongue. My heart beat faster, but I strove to calm it. I have never been given to a belief in the supernatural. This primitive fear that now crept over me would not beat my nerves. I was a man of science, and a man of science I would remain.

Tentatively, I spoke out, 'Hello?' My words hung unanswered.

Trying to make sense of what I heard, I thought perhaps some unfortunate and fallen and lay now injured among the sepulchres calling with what strength remained to him, unable to voice his needs any louder. I called again, but no sensible reply came to my shout, just the repeated whispering. It haunted the place, a susurration, a muttering. My unease grew. I cleared my throat and called again. Now I suspected some trickster, and I told myself if they did not answer this second time, I would leave.

I had no wish to enter the churchyard with its countless graves and shadows no matter how rational a man I might be in daylight, but my duty as a doctor bore upon me to tend to the injured. Duty called me to go into the graveyard, but I did not step through the gate. I half turned. I half took a step away, but guilt clawed at me. Despite my earlier mind to call out only twice, I shouted a third time. Still no answer came.

I made my mind up that I must enter the churchyard to check for anyone that might need my help, but, as I put my hand to the iron gate, the whispering fell suddenly silent. A minute of dead silence was enough to reassure me that no one lay wounded and in need.

With a sense of relief, I continued the few yards to Appleby's House. His housekeeper opened the door — a thin-lipped, pock-marked woman in a black costume reminiscent of, and probably a remnant of, those worn by upper house servants fifty years ago. She muttered, 'I'm glad to see you here, Dr Graham. The Reverend is not well. I'm happy you've come.'

She wittered anxiously in front of me all the way up the stairs to the first floor where Appleby had his room. The housekeeper opened the door into a room lit by hissing gas mantles under glass shades. The room was warm and smelled of sickness. Shelves and shelves of old books lined each wall, and heavy curtains to the front hid the window.

Looking around, it seemed Reverend Appleby had chosen to retire to his library rather than his bedroom. The room was untidy with a mahogany writing desk heaped with papers and old books, pens and a large inkwell. Further books littered the floor in piles, spilling every-where, some opened and laid face down as if he feared to lose his place in them and had not enough bookmarks.

Appleby sat up in a chair, his blankets thrown off, beads of sweat standing proud from his creased forehead. He coughed weakly as he attempted to greet me. Beside him, I noticed a china bowl, a chamber pot by the look of it, but put now to the use of catching his respiratory exudations.

I said, 'Good evening, Reverend Appleby. How can I help you?'

'I haven't called you to treat my illness, if that's what you think' he said before speech was extinguished by a wracking cough. A brief glance showed me the chamber pot now contained more phlegm streaked with frank blood.

He didn't want me to treat his illness? Peculiar to summon a doctor to his house to greet me with that, but I put it down to him being confused. From a glance alone, it seemed clear what was wrong with him.

Sir Dyce Duckworth has lectured on the treatment of pneumonia. As he notes, historically we have treated it by bleeding, reduced diet and application of mercury or calomel but studies from Vienna show a better survival rate with dieting and rest rather than the use of repeated bleeding and toxic drugs. I had hoped that better treatments would come from further study of the streptococcus and staphylococcus bacteria, but so far we have to work with such remedies as we have to hand.

He wasn't able to breathe well enough to protest further, so I examined him. On observation, he had a productive cough and the blood would be explained by tears in the lung membrane arising from mechanical shearing during coughing. On auscultation, I heard low pitched crackles in the base of both lungs. On percussion, dullness suggesting consolidation. Pneumonia, very likely. All physicians know the danger of diagnostic foreclosure, but I was fairly confident of my diagnosis. 'Reverend Appleby,' I said. 'I fear you have pneumonia. But do not worry, I propose a treatment'

Appleby seized my forearm. His grip was weak. He was agitated and anxious to speak, but his intended words were disrupted by an extended bout of coughing. Eyes watering, he put his handkerchief to his mouth and doubled forward in his seat as I stepped back. There was blood again on his handkerchief when at last he said, 'This is no ordinary infection, Dr Graham.'

It looked like pneumonia to me. 'Whatever can you mean, Appleby? I assure you—'

With a hand, he waved me down. 'No, doctor, it is not a natural ailment. I did not catch my final illness from another human being.'

I frowned, impatient at his dismissal of my diagnosis. For all his bluster, I did not see where he was leading with his comments, and felt his resistance was merely delaying treatment, but he seemed determined to have his say, so I sighed and nodded. 'Then, pray tell me, Reverend Appleby, from where did you catch it?'

He gave a dry laugh, broken off with more coughing and gestured with a weak hand to the pile of books on his desk. One, a narrow tome, old and bound in stained red leather, lay aside from the others as if sequestered from them for fear it might infect them too with its strange disease.

I raised an eyebrow. 'A book? You can scarcely mean you caught it from a book?' I looked at him again, wondering whether his fever had induced a delirium.

Appleby sat back, his lips tinged blue. He could hardly speak. 'Yes. A book. You find it hard to believe?'

I shrugged. 'If you mean, traces of infection were on the book and you picked it up that way, then perhaps...'

He shook his head. 'I do not mean that, good doctor. I mean the book contains the illness.'

I scratched my earlobe. 'I'm not sure I follow you, Appleby. And in any case, I need to proceed with treatment.' I had my bulky leather doctor's bag with me placed at my feet. I unlocked it and delved within thinking to find something to help him with, but Appleby said, 'As I said, I did not ask you here to treat me, doctor. I fear I am beyond that.'

Irritated, I stood askance. 'Then why did you ask me?'

His eyes were down as he continued. 'Dr Graham, you are a man of science, and you have the reputation in the local area as being a man of your word.'

I said, 'I should I hope I do. And I must say, it is gratifying that you have that impression of me.'

He interrupted me. 'I need you to take that cursed book and destroy it.'

I paused. 'Destroy it? Is it not valuable?' I glanced over. Certainly it looked antique.

'Valuable? It is damnation, sir. Pure damnation.'

'Ah,' I said. Certainly he was delirious. He coughed again so hard I thought it would be the end of him. I stepped closer, but he put up a feeble hand. 'Please, I do not want treatment. I am ready to die. Indeed, I deserve to die for my damned curiosity. Those wiser in these things than me warned me, but I didn't listen. I obtained and then, to my cost, read the *Liber Officiorum Spirituum*.

'The Book of the Spirits' Office?' My Latin was serviceable. I studied it at school, and of course at medical college, but my translation made me no wiser. I asked him where he got it.

'From a tomb.'

'A tomb?' He confabulated, surely. 'What on earth would a book be doing in a tomb?'

'A man took it with him to the grave, a doctor like yourself, James Gwinne, who died in 1627 and is buried next door at St Anne's. I should have left it with him.'

'A doctor, you say?'

'Aye, a physician, but one hungry for knowledge, and who paid dearly for it. The book was buried with him because his followers feared it; feared that it be read, but also feared to destroy it. The book contains secrets — secrets obtained from supernatural powers by unnatural means.'

'What on earth is it about?'

'It is about disease, doctor. But the diseases it concerns are diseases of the soul as well as the body. They can infect from words alone.'

I was sceptical. 'Are you suggesting that mere words in a book gave you this ailment?'

Appleby nodded. 'Dr Gwinne was a genius, but he entered into a pact with the forces of darkness. They gave him this book. In his time, he was regarded as a miracle worker. But such bargains have to be kept and such knowledge paid for. Each time he used a cure, the book took the disease into itself until at last it was filled with illness.'

'You say that the words of the book have filled with disease and are now infective?'

'I say that. Each disease he cured, entered into the pages of the book until they ultimately overflowed with illness.'

'Preposterous.'

'No, Dr Graham, reading the words alone is enough to infect a man. The disease comes into his soul through his eyes and no human remedy can cure it.' Appleby coughed again, then went on. 'My strength is fading now, I have little time to discuss this further. All I ask, doctor, is that you take this book and burn it. I lack the strength both mental and physical now to destroy the damned thing.'

He began to cough again. This time his handkerchief had more blood. His eyes were sunken, his cheeks hollow and his lips blue. From experience, I knew he had little time to live.

I moved closer. 'Please, let me attempt to treat you.'

But by the time I'd spoken, he was dead. I called the housekeeper who was wracked with tears. 'He was a good man, many didn't think so, but he was good to me,' she said between her sobs.

I pronounced life extinct at just after 11 pm. She left me alone in the room for a while and I went to the desk where the book lay, quiet and innocuous. I didn't touch it, just observed. How curious. Appleby believed the mere words of a book could kill a man. This was clearly impossible. Without doubt, Appleby had been prey to delusions brought on by his final illness.

I touched the book tentatively. I don't know what I expected. It felt normal enough. The leather was old and stained as if it had lain locked in many libraries over many years. There was a stain of clay too, as if it had been buried. From the side, I saw the pages were of parchment, not paper. On the front, in much younger tooling, as if added years after the book was first made, were letters that read: *Liber Officiorum Spirituum* in faded gold.

I lifted it. It felt heavy in my hand. I was turning it when I thought I heard a sound emanate from it. Instantly, I slammed it down on the table. As it lay there, I heard a faint whispering again. I put that down to the wind. But there was no wind that night.

Interrupting my musings, the housekeeper came back with an envelope.

'What's this?' I asked as she tried to thrust it into my grasp.

'Your fee.'

I shook my head. 'I did nothing. I wish I could have helped him, but it was too late.'

'He instructed me to give you it.'

'Please, you keep it.'

But she wouldn't have it and just to placate her, I took it, but when she left the room again going about the many things she had to do now her master was gone, I placed the envelope with its money on the desk besides the *Liber Officiorum Spirituum*. I looked at that book for a long time, then glanced back to the deceased Appleby. Destroy it? I must admit I had a fancy to read the words of this Dr Gwinne, to see whether he were such a genius as Appleby claimed.

I was alone in the house. The housekeeper had gone to call the Undertaker. I would leave them the death certificate. It was late. I was tired. I decided I would take the book, but I would not burn it. Once we got past all the superstitious nonsense, we might find some worthwhile medical knowledge.

I grasped the book and placed it in my doctor's bag. It felt strangely warm to the touch as if the leather had been warmed by a fire, though it was near no source of heat. An irrational thought occurred to me that perhaps the book had some life of its own; some self-generated heat.

I turned at the door, looking back at Appleby's corpse, blue-grey and waxen. In my imagination, I half saw some kind of worm slip under his shirt. I started back. In my fatigued state, I thought more worms coiled from his mouth and fell onto his clothes. In a panic, I ran out and slammed the door behind me. I was becoming prey to hallucinations. Leaving his house, I set off for home.

By the gate to St Ann's Church, I listened out for the sound I had heard earlier. But it was quiet — a strange, full silence that lurked there in shadows as if something out of sight watched. The ghost of Dr James Gwinne, I wondered. I shuddered and continued home. The fog was thicker now, and my footfall echoed. I met no one but a policeman with a bull's eye lantern who bid me good night.

Finally in my own house, I retired to my study to think over the evening's events. I lived with my wife Mary and three children, but they were visiting her family in Winchester and so I was left in my Soho House, not far from the Square. Drybone my manservant had retired to bed with my permission after providing a plate of cold ham and mustard cut by his own hand now the cook and maids were asleep. I sat with a whisky in my study. Medical textbooks lined the shelves. The fire whispered to itself in the hearth and in front of me, on the desk, lay the *Liber Officiorum Spirituum*.

I could throw it on the fire right now. But what use would that be? I must admit my academic curiosity took my hand to open it, but then I stopped. I chided myself for that. Appleby's delusions were infecting me, making me scared. I sipped my whisky and water, gazed at the book, and pondered.

Appleby had told me not to look inside it. He had claimed that looking inside it was the thing that had brought that infection. How could that be? How could words become the bearers of disease?

I tapped my finger on the leather binding, traced the name with my fingertip, but still did not open it. Such foolishness. My whisky glass was empty. I went to the table in the corner where the decanter stood and a jug of water and poured myself a generous measure. I stood, glass in hand, looking slyly over my shoulder at the book, perhaps fearing it might even open itself and the sickness pour out?

It was late. I was tired. Soon I would retire to bed. I would just finish this drink.

I put down my glass and placed more coals on the fire as the foggy night outside had chilled me. At least, I thought it was the fog that chilled me rather than the memory of Appleby and his deranged ramblings. How could a man think a mere book could bring about his death? And an intelligent man at that: a scholar? I poked the coals, stirring up blue and yellow flames. The warmth was pleasing.

Done with the poker, I took up my whisky and sipped. All the while, I stood watching the book, then I went to up the desk and stood, regarding it. The Book of the Offices of the Spirits. It had got the name, no doubt because the ignorant had thought it some kind of demonological tome. But learned men in earlier times were often thought to be wizards and necromancers. The book had got a bad name because it contained knowledge too elevated for those who were not trained. That was what explained the superstitious dread attached to it. I doubt even Appleby would have understood it. He was a learned man, surely, in Theology and other such subjects. But I was a medical man. Of course the information in this book would mean more to me than to him.

I sighed. Took another dram of whisky and pursed my lips. I would just look inside. What harm could that do? Just a glimpse. And so I opened the Book of the Offices of the Spirits.

The black ink of the words had faded brown, and the letters were angular. I rubbed my eyes, and cursed my tiredness. The words seemed to move and shift under my gaze. I turned the pages: lists of diseases and remedies, called by old-fashioned names, mostly unfamiliar to me. I translated,

'All things are poison, and nothing is without poison; the dosage alone makes it so a thing is not a poison.'

That was from Paracelsus.
I read on.

"All healing arises from this foul blackness, and the blackness takes the sickness unto itself. But take care, fill not overfull the words of this book, for they will spill over and poison he who reads them."

I tutted. More superstition.

With my finger tracing the lines to keep them steady, I read the words that spoke of the matrix and the healing tincture. Some of it was meaningful to me. I read of pneumonia and melancholia, of the juice of milk thistle and of nightshade. I heard my voice speaking the words out loud, but this was not under my control, my words chattered without me willing them to. It was as if the book was taking me over. I heard syllables arise in my throat, glide over my teeth, form themselves in the tapping of my tongue, until the words were out in the room; in the air before me. And once out of my mouth, the disease formed itself as a miasma in the air.

As I gazed on, horrified, it seemed to me that worms emerged from the book, squirming from between the ancient pages. Squirming and writhing and falling softly to the floor. I jumped back, upsetting the whisky glass, knocking it against the side of the desk. The worms wriggled on the rug, they slithered onto to my shoes and wrapped around my ankles. There were hundreds of them. They wound and climbed up up my calves and my thighs and I tried to beat them off, frantically trying to stop them coming to my neck or chin and entering my mouth. And the foul brown vapour that emerged from the book's fluttering pages, entered my mouth, and I inhaled it into my lungs where it burned and bubbled, smothering my breath.

I called out for Drybone. I sat down heavily, choking in my seat. Fever rose in me as the disease stole my air. My heart beat wildly for life, and I grew clammy with sweat. My muscles spasmed agonisingly. I was so weak I could hardly move. The disease possessed and grew in me until I flopped, limp, my head down, coughing up blood, my breath bubbling through the brown moisture that filled my airways.

With my last strength, I again called for my servant Drybone. But Drybone is healthy and always sleeps deep.

I call again, but my voice is weak. He cannot hear me.

I am dying now. Still help has not come.

❅ 5 ❅

THE LIFT

Sometimes you can't tell when you're dreaming. That's really scary. But when you can't wake up, that's worse.

The night was cold and dark and I lay alone in my bed with a ghastly old woman draping dirty hair over my face, her weight squashing my chest and coming in to kiss me with spittle-flecked lips. I went to shove her off. 'Get away from me!'

But she cackled and came in again, whispering, 'Give yer granny a snog!'

I screamed and heaved her off me so hard she tumbled from the bed, cracking her head on the floor. I jumped up, the bed sheets tangling my legs, terrified I'd killed her, but when I looked, there was no one on the floor. The old woman wasn't there.

My gaze darted around my bedroom, scared she might be dead, more scared she might still be there. But she wasn't.

I breathed hard, trying to calm myself, still sweating. Street light poured in through the slits in my blinds, liquid orange-red. The old woman was truly gone. It was just a dream, but it had felt so real. I laughed nervously. So real I'd thought the old woman was actually in the room, sitting on me, trying to kiss me.

Sweat soaked the t-shirt I wore, now drying and making me cold.

The warp and woof of dreams still wrapped around my head. My mind knew she wasn't real, never had been real, but my body still reacted as if she might reappear at any moment.

I walked through to the kitchen to get a glass of water. The kitchen felt strange and unfamiliar, but I told myself this was just the tattered rags of dream persisting. I sipped the water. The glass felt smooth and warm in my fingers. This was real. This was really real and I had to get some sleep. I had an interview the next day. With my brain still fugged, I struggled to remember what the interview was for. I couldn't recall, but best not to worry, details would come back after a little more sleep.

I awoke to the pulse of the alarm, grey light seeping into the room. I had no time to lie in bed. It was probably this that was making me anxious and had caused the dream. The dream and the interview were certainly linked.

On the Docklands Light Railway train, drifting off, I suddenly realised that Stefan from work sat on the seat opposite me. I hadn't noticed him get on the train. I looked up from my phone and he was staring at me.

'Stefan?' I said, 'What are you doing here?'

'I've got an interview,' he said, an enormous grin on his chubby face.

Weird that he'd got an interview too. It couldn't be for the same job as mine. I was a marketer; he was a software dude.

Stefan was sweaty and old and his suit was too tight. He had a folder in his thick hands, like he had made notes. It had the number 52 scrawled on it. His hands looked like mine.

I don't remember whether he got off at the same stop as me. I was too preoccupied with the interview. I remembered now that the interview was for a sales job, but for the life of me, I couldn't remember the name of the company. I exhaled. I needed to clear my head. This was stupid. I needed to focus if I was to stand a chance of getting the job.

Still, I was normally good at interviews. I just hoped I could hold it together.

The wind blew wintry over the water and the leaves in the park rattled brown and withered as the year headed to its death.

As I walked beside the River Thames, the waves were grey and tossed as if by inner anxiety. They mirrored my own inner disquiet as I couldn't shake the feeling of strangeness.

I lit a cigarette while I stood there in the plaza. Crone Holdings, a weird name for a company. Must have been started by a Mr Crone. I remembered there was a Crone's Tailors in my hometown when I was a boy. Shut now.

The insurance company building rose like a stone needle into the sky and in there would be a lift. I hoped the interview was on the ground floor or at least not at the top because I had a fear of lifts. I'd had it since I was a kid. I could never get rid of the image of being trapped in a steel box suspended between floors with no way out. Maybe it was some subconscious fear of being consumed, but I was always so embarrassed about the weakness that I told no one about it.

Time ticked on. I finally couldn't put things off any further so I gave a last drag on the cigarette and flipped the butt, watching it spin and land between the straggly roots of half-starved weeds.

Crone Holding's skyscraper doors were wide but somehow unwelcoming. As I stepped up, the glass doors opened with a hiss like a breath.

I walked up to the reception desk while the guards spoke on phones, capped in black with shiny peaks, wearing quasi-military uniforms. They made me wait, but they had to let me in because I had an interview.

I looked into the lobby and saw a bank of lifts in the far wall. My heart flipped over and I hoped my weakness didn't show to those men sitting there in judgement with their shiny black caps. One of them was staring like he knew what was going on in my head. I forced a smile, but he didn't smile back. Then he put down the phone and nodded at me to wait in the seats by the water cooler. I did as I was told and sat down on a plush leather sofa, thinking of picking up a copy of *Autocar* or *World Traveller*, until a secretary came down to get me. Her black pencil skirt hugged her curves and contrasted with her white blonde hair. I smiled, but she was impassive. She was cold as ice cream but not so sweet.

The blonde secretary said, "Upstairs will let us know when they're ready for you to go up in the lift." She stood there for a second, as if waiting for a question.   I had none; I was focused on her words — *up in the lift*. I ran my finger round the inside of my shirt collar. I wished I could loosen my tie.

I stared at the lift door, and then glanced away, but it kept pulling my gaze, and every second I stared, I felt worse.

Ten minutes went by. I sat looking at my shoes, my fingers, the table, anything but the lift.

Finally the Ice Blonde returned. I grinned sheepishly, trying to win her as an ally but she repelled my gaze. She said, "They've rung down." She looked at me as if I might not understand and added, "Upstairs have rung down."

I nodded. She reminded me of someone.

I got up. She pointed to the elevator. "Fifty-second floor."

Oh hell, that was a long lift journey.

She let me walk ahead of her and when we got to the elevator doors; she waited. I waited for her to press the call button, but she didn't. So I had to. I felt my stomach turn over.

I stared at the panel above the lift to see how long I had before I had to get into that box. It was coming down fast. Then the lift pinged as it arrived.

"There. Fifty-second floor, remember," she said. She was turning to go. I suddenly realised she looked like my cousin Jenny. I hadn't seen Jenny in years. I almost asked if it was her, but Jenny lived in Canada now. It couldn't be Jenny.

The lift door stood, metal doors wide open.

"Aren't you coming up with me?" I said.

She shook her head without speaking and walked off.

I caught my smeared reflection in the door's steel and saw that I was dressed as if I'd walked out of a cheap competitor of GQ Magazine. So what? My suit wasn't expensive, but it was clean and sharp. My shoes shone. That morning, I'd put on my best shirt, ironed by my laundry lady, and I wore the eighteen-carat gold cuff-links given to me by my grandfather on the day I got my first job.

The lift doors hissed; the mirror at the back of the lift welcomed me in like it was hungry.

I gulped and stepped in. I had to. The guards and the blonde were watching me, I was sure of it. Inside, I adjusted my tie. I swallowed. My eyes bulged a little.

"It'll be okay," I whispered to myself. "It's just a job interview."

The doors closed.

I pressed the button for the 52nd Floor.

Fifty-two is a lot of floors.

The doors took a lifetime to close and while they came slowly to; I tapped repeatedly on the button for the fifty-second floor until it lit up with a tasteful blue light. Doors now closed, panic rose. I tried to push it down.

The elevator shifted as if preparing for the ascent. Then up it shot. Gravity rooted me to the floor. My stomach lifted with the sharp acceleration.

Sweat beaded on my forehead. I felt sick. It wasn't the speed that made me sick; it was the thought of not getting out again.

Weird, this lift was just like the one in Hambro's when I worked there when I was seventeen and I lived at my grandma's. Almost exactly the same. That's when my phobia of lifts started, that time I got stuck in there with the old lady.

Still shooting up, the lift's cabin light flickered but then came back on strongly. That scared me. I thought it would stop.

My heart pulsed in my ears. It moved too fast — I imagined the lift failing to stop and bursting out of the top of the tower. I told myself to calm down. It was perfectly safe. The sooner it got there, the sooner I'd be free of the box.   I pulled out a cotton handkerchief and wiped my brow.

"Thirty-three," said Stefan. "Still a long way to go." He sighed heavily. "I get claustrophobic."

I said nothing.

He cleared his throat. "You know what, Mark? I'd prefer to walk."

Stefan stood there with me in the lift. I had only the slightest thought that it was odd he was there.

I tried to make my voice sound normal. "Trust me; you wouldn't like to walk up twenty odd floors." I looked him over. Stefan didn't go to the gym. His little pot belly hung over his black leather belt, held back by his clean blue shirt. That made me feel better because I was in better shape than him.

He laughed, seeing my gaze and patting his stomach. "No, Mark. I guess you're right."

The lift settled, as if preparing itself, then a pause before the door hissed open, revealing a modern, clean, spiritless corridor. We waited for someone to come, but the corridor was empty and still. It was as if the thirty-third floor was uninhabited. The doors closed again, like the curtains closing on a play where nothing happens.

Stefan smiled at me.

I tried to make a joke to calm my nerves. "Busy here, huh? Maybe the entire building is empty. No one works here; it's just for show."

Stefan frowned. "But we have an appointment."

"Don't take me so literally."

"Ah," he said.

I frowned. "Do you have the papers?"

He tapped his shiny attaché case. "On my laptop." I thought he had a file, but that was gone now. He must have left it somewhere.

"What if the laptop doesn't work...?"

He grinned and reached out to give my arm a reassuring squeeze. "Don't fret, Mark."

I looked at his pale fingers on my suit; I could see the pink of the nail beds. I wanted him to take his hand off my arm. "I'm not fretting."

It wasn't an interview I was going for. I don't know why I'd ever thought that. I remembered now that Stefan and I had actually been asked to a sales pitch for a contract.

The lift moved again with the same sensation of taking off as we hurtled upwards.

Then it stopped.

My heart fluttered.

"What the fuck?" Stefan yelled. He hugged his attaché case to him like a shield. If he was scared, I couldn't let my terror show.

I coughed. "Don't worry. It'll start again in a minute."

We waited more than a minute. I ran my hand through my hair. It was wet. Stefan started looking around the elevator cabin like a frightened rabbit. His eyes took in the control panel with its alarm. He looked at the ceiling but there was no exit hatch like there is in the movies.

"Honestly, it should start soon," I said.

He was wild-eyed. "We'll be late."

I said, "They must know their own lift is stuck."

He said, "It didn't sound like it broke; it just stopped."

"But we're between floors."

He nodded insistently. "It just stopped; like it meant to."

"Lifts don't have intentions, Stefan." My tone was too sharp, but he grinned at me apologetically.

"Should we press the alarm?" he said finally.

We definitely should, but I didn't want to look like the weaker one. I shrugged. "It'll start going in a minute."

Then the light went off. I heard myself make a noise. The cabinet was pitch-black. I pressed my hand onto the warm metal wall just to prove to myself it was still there.

"Don't worry, Mark," Stefan said, putting his hand on my back. "I can see you're scared. You're trying to hide it but I know. I know you."

I could see the light from the control panels and it showed me Stefan's suited form huddled against the wall, clutching his attaché case.

"I'm pressing the alarm," I stammered.

"I'll do it if you like," he said.

He leaned in front of me and pushed the button. Somewhere, silently, the alarm went off. Or at least, I hoped it did.

I rubbed my clammy forehead. What the hell was I even doing in this building? Something about a pitch for a job? I didn't even work with Stefan. Why were we here together?

I sat, my back pressed against the smooth steel wall. The floor buttons glowed orange. I had my elbows on my knees and was clutching my head. Stefan sat in the other corner, his head bowed. It was now five minutes since we pressed the alarm and no one had come. The floor buttons continued to glow softly.

Stefan said, "Do you think someone will come soon?"

"I hope so."

"They should come soon, though," Stefan said.

"Yeah."

"I mean, they'll have heard the alarm."

"Yep."

"They wouldn't just leave us, would they?"

I was adding his anxiety to mine. I needed to get out of that damned metal box.

He paused. "They're probably out there now. Can you hear them?"

I couldn't but I nodded, the sweat dripping over my lip

"Yes, it's going to be alright," he said.

My chest felt tight; I coughed.

"You okay?" he said.

"Yep."

"Okay." He stood up, went, and looked at the floor buttons. "Should I press it again?"

"Do." I heard the snap in my voice.

He pressed it. "Still no sound."

"Fuck's sake, Stefan."

"Hmm," he said. "Guess we'll just have to wait."

He sat down again and was mercifully silent. My finger ends tingled with fear.

Then the lift moved. "Thank God," I said.

The lift jerked as if preparing to go up or down. I jumped to my feet and hit the buttons randomly. My shirt was wringing wet.

Stefan came and put a reassuring hand on my back. "Don't worry, Markie, we'll get out." The hand lay there like an unwelcome guest. I felt the fingers across my shoulder blades. It felt familiar. Then the elevator went down. I breathed out. The main cabin light still didn't come on, but at least it was moving.

"Hey, it's going down," Stefan said.

I nodded, my forehead pressed against the metal wall.

We were heading rapidly down to the ground floor. I thought of the entrance lobby with its faceless, self-congratulatory suits and the Ice Blonde bitch secretary, my cousin Jenny. How much I wanted the doors to open and to be out there.

The light indicated we had arrived at the first floor. I exhaled and relaxed, my anxiety going out of me like a deflating balloon. I straightened my tie and regretted the damp sweat mark on my collar. The lift settled. The doors gave a preparatory hum.   Then the doors opened to reveal, not the brightly lit glass and steel lobby we had come from, but nothing.

Outside the lift door was a complete void.

This didn't make sense.

Panic surged up.

The darkness out there had no gradient, no darker shadows, no silhouettes; it was uniformly grey-black of the darkest hue. It was as if there was nothing there at all, but it wasn't empty, it was like a space pregnant with meaning, like a negative waiting for the developing tray.

It felt vacant, malign and hungry.

I reached into my jacket pocket and drew out my phone. I pressed the screen and clean white light spilled out into the grey-black world but I could make nothing out; I wasn't even sure that there was a floor to walk on. The only sense I could make of it was that somehow the lights had gone out. This was the ground floor. The ground floor led onto the street.

And then I heard low growling.

"What's that?" I heard the panic in Stefan's voice.

I stammered, "I don't know."

"Is it dogs?" he said.

"Dogs? Why dogs?" I hated dogs too. Terrified of them since my grandma's Alsatian bit me when I was five.

He nodded. "Guard dogs. Maybe they've unleashed them because the building is on lockdown. Maybe there are intruders."

I didn't need dogs. I said, "This is an office block, not a high security prison. Why would they unleash animals on people locked in a building?"

"Maybe it's not dogs."

"Maybe."

"It sounded like dogs." Then he turned with a weird smile. "Maybe it's things worse than dogs."

That really freaked me. I swallowed hard. "Things worse than dogs, what do you mean?"

Stefan didn't answer. Now he seemed to find the whole situation very amusing.

The growling came closer. I pushed myself back into the elevator. I couldn't see a dog out there in the dark, but I was scared one might jump at me from out of nowhere. I hit the button and closed the doors.

The lift moved upwards as rapidly as when we first entered it. My stomach heaved as it took off.

The cabin was still dim, but my eyes were used to it now. There was actually an intercom. I hadn't noticed it before. I pressed the red glowing button and held it. "Hello," I said. This is Mark Krawitz. I'm in your elevator. I'm here for a meeting with your finance director."

That seemed right. I thought I was there for a meeting with the finance director, but suddenly, I wasn't sure.

No one replied.

The hurtling lift slowed as we neared our destination. We stopped at the 52nd Floor. My heart skipped as I waited for the doors to open, but they didn't open.

A noise came from the intercom, faint and rushing like the soft whistling you get when you place a seashell to your ear. We used to live at the seaside.

"It's saying something," Stefan said.

"I can't hear any words."

"No, listen."

The noise got louder. Then I made out distant singing, but not tuneful and whatever music it was supposed to be was mixed in with bursts of interference and white noise as if it was coming from somewhere very far away.

"What's it saying?" I listened with my full concentration. I couldn't make it out.

He didn't reply.

'Stefan,' I asked. 'What's it's saying?'

He was smiling. "It's saying 'Grandmother is waiting.'"

I put my hand to my throat. "Grandma's waiting." I stammered. "What does that mean? Grandmother's waiting?"

Then the doors opened.

I didn't move.

Stefan said, "You're late for your appointment."

He gestured for me to go first, like he was being generous.

There was a long corridor in front, just a normal corridor. Windows and pictures lined it.   I couldn't make out what the pictures were of, ordinary landscapes I think. At the end of the passage was a double door of polished wood.

Stefan nodded conspiratorially towards the closed doors. "She's waiting for you."

The place felt flat and without resonance, unreal somehow, like it was a set in a movie.

I walked. I looked to my left and saw the grey skyscraper teeth of the city through the windows and I heard what I thought was the wail of its endless police cars, or of the wind. The fog licked the windows, trying to get in.

The corridor had rich red patterned carpets: diamonds and hearts. They reminded me of the pack of cards my grandmother had, when she taught me to play that game.

"Hurry, Markie," Stefan said.

"Wait a minute. " I just wanted to buy time. I had no tie and my shirt was stained with sweat.

Stefan raised an eyebrow.

"I just need to compose myself before meeting the Finance Director."

He shook his head. "It's not the Finance Director who's in there."

I said, "But we're here to see the Finance Director, to make the deal, remember."

Stefan stood there smiling.

I heard the clip clop of high heels from behind as the ice-blonde receptionist, my cousin, Jenny, joined us. She had always stayed at grandma's with us at 52 Sea View.

"Jenny, what are you doing here?"

She ignored me. "Do you remember what happened there, Mark?
"

"Where?"

"At grandma's."

I shook my head. I couldn't remember anything. It was like a fog had descended on me.

"She told us the secret."

"The secret?"

Jenny nodded insistently. "And Stefan."

"Stefan, who I work with?"

"You don't work with Stefan," Jenny said.

"I don't know," I said. I was confused.

She took my arm and squeezed it. "Don't you remember Uncle Stefan? My dad. Your mum's brother."

Yes, I remembered. Mum's weird brother Stefan. My uncle. My mother hated him, but she'd died and we'd had to go to grandma's where he was. I spun round and saw it really was fat Uncle Stefan. He smiled. His lips were wet. There was something I had to remember. Something frightening.

Jenny said, "Don't think you can wake up, Mark. There is no waking world."

"I don't belong here," I said. "I want to leave. I don't want this job."

Jenny stared at me. "Whatever you think, Mark, you've always been with us."

I had a vague memory of it all. Nightmares in mirrors reflecting one another without end.

"It's time, Mark."

"Time, Markie," Uncle Stefan said. "On you go."

Jenny pushed me onward.

I paused, looking at the polished wooden door that hadn't opened yet. "Who's in there?"

Jenny reached over and smoothed my hair like I was a little boy. "Get ready."   Then she nodded. "She's waiting for you."

Stefan opened the door. The room inside was large and the light came from stones on the ground, an evil light, like that which comes from dead fish. The walls weren't of wood or stone; they were made of flesh, glistening flesh hung all around, moving, gurgling, and thinking.

"I don't want to go in," I said.

Jinny and Stefan both laughed, real belly laughs, they doubled up in mirth.

Beyond the door, standing in the middle of the room, with her back to us, was an old woman. She was hunched and wore a heavy shawl on her head so I couldn't see her hair. If I saw her hair, I knew I'd recognise her.

"Do you remember this place?" said Stefan.

Jenny studied her nails.

I shook my head. "I've never been here before."

"Really? You really think that?" He laughed.

Jenny said, "You always think that. Time to remember."

In front of me, the old woman shook like she had a neurological condition. Just like grandma. I knew she was waiting to turn round, waiting for Stefan to say the secret words.

My hands shook. "Who is this woman?"

"You know," Jenny said.

Stefan smiled; his eyes were false; his teeth were false; his face was someone else's. He wasn't really Stefan. Jenny wasn't really Jenny. That was the secret.

I swallowed, but my throat had closed. I thought I'd choke.

I was closer to the old woman now. I heard her breathing. Her hands were outstretched but her head was still bowed, still hung with the heavy shawl. The old woman turned, her filthy ragged hair hanging lank and loose. She grinned, showing yellow teeth. Her rubbery lips were wet.

"Come and give yer granny a snog!" she reached out, grinning.

❦   6   ❦

A LETTER FROM THE DEAD

It was May Day and we were young and dawn had come up on us by surprise as we left a party in Camden and Simon said, 'Let's walk up Primrose Hill and watch the sun rise over London.'

We always did what he said. There was me, him and Sofia, his girl-friend. She was half Italian, half Scottish — a heady mix, and she was beautiful and I loved her. The problem was she loved Simon and Simon loved her right back, so I kept my feelings under wraps. He was my brother after all.

That morning, we were still half drunk and drugged. We shared a bottle of vodka passing it from lips to lips, and as we saw the golden, orange globe heave itself over Kent, Simon suddenly said, 'Let's swear an oath!' and took a mouthful of vodka like it was a toast to the morning, or a toast to the rest of our lives.

He was into his Shelley, Byron, Classical phase then and he said, 'Let us swear by the Furies that we shall be forever true!'

'True to who?' I said.

'To each other!'

'To each other!' Sofia yelled into the bright air, hands thrown up.

Simon said, 'We love each other. Let us swear that we will never let each other down.'

'I swear!' Sofia said.

'Yeah, of course,' I said.

'Swear!' Simon repeated. I knew him when he was intense like this, he couldn't be put off. 'Okay,' I said finally. 'I swear.'

'By the Furies!' he said.

I nodded. 'By the Furies'

'Who are the Furies?' Sofia asked.

'Just swear,' I whispered, 'Keep him happy.'

She laughed. 'I swear by the Furies too!'

Just words. Just drunken words.

FIVE YEARS LATER, I WAS WALKING DOWN CAMDEN HIGH STREET when I remembered him. The sun emerged from behind a cloud and doused the street in the butter yellow of late summer light. I was just near the place we'd started drinking that night. The time and weather were even the same. But not me. I wasn't the same. I'd changed my ways; I got a job in a coffee shop. I had a badge and an apron and I even paid my taxes. Instead of squatting in the houses of friend after friend, I rented a small apartment not far from the canal. Most important, I didn't do drugs anymore: these days I managed my emotions, not through chemicals, but by meditation and going to the gym.

There was sweat on the back of my neck. I remembered sweating that night. I still remember the smell of tar melted in the London sun, the tang of petrol and the tickle of pollution at the back of my throat. I remembered everything. That was the night Simon died.

But now, after my Camden High Street reverie, I walked on, glad to shake off the sense of unease his death still gave me. It was Saturday. I wandered down to the Lock and made my way through the hordes of leather jacketed neo-punks, leavened as they were with the yeast of wondering wandering tourists. I strolled past the Mexican and Thai food stalls, steam rising from the rice, the aromas almost enticing me to eat, past stalls selling jewellery made of mother boards encased in resin, past the incense sellers and the shops pushing books at people angry with the status quo, past it all. I walked with nowhere in mind. The only thing I wanted was to be past the past. Whenever it rose up in memory, I pushed it down again.

And then a thunderbolt struck: I saw Sofia again, after all this time and she was still beautiful. So beautiful she stopped me dead and I couldn't help but stare. Memories made my heart trip and flip. She wore a black motorcycle jacket and black jeans. Her hair was long and black, glossy over her shoulders as she bent into a friend to light a cigarette. Then with cigarette lit, she leaned back, inhaled and blew out a twisting cloud of blue smoke. From the laughter, she was telling a joke I couldn't hear. Her girlfriend put her hand to her mouth to stifle the giggle and then Sofia looked around, her pupils shifting like a camera on auto-focus, going this way and that until she had me sharp. There was a moment's hesitation; her brain processing whether I really was the long-lost Luke. Then a smile. I smiled back, almost without meaning to.

I pushed my hand through my hair. I thought I didn't want her to walk over. Then, as she came, I realised I did. There she stood in the sunshine, like a memory of a wish, if there could be such a thing. Her beauty wasn't just classical, it was haunting as well. She stood before me. "Luke, my God, you're still here!"

I cleared my throat. "Yeah, In Camden. I never moved." I felt stiff and awkward.

She leaned up and kissed me on the cheek without being asked. She said. "We haven't seen each other since…" And then she remembered.

I said, "Yeah."

She said, "Ah."

A shadow passed behind her eyes. She said, "I can't forget it."

I shrugged. "Why would you?"

"I don't want to forget…" she said.

I didn't reply. "Anyway…" I glanced back over my shoulder like there was somewhere I had to be.

"Let's go for a drink," she blurted.

"Well…"

"If it's not convenient…" She looked almost uncertain. Not like the Sofia I remembered.

"You back in Camden?" I asked.

"Chalk Farm."

A pause. "Nice."

She said, "It's a friend's place. They're away for the summer. It's better than I could afford."

"Where've you been?" I said.

"In between."

She reached out and touched my arm. I let her fingers lie, but didn't move closer. "Why not come for a drink, and I'll tell you?"

I almost made an excuse. She always haunted me and now she stood there in black, a revenant.

"Come on." She walked towards The World's End, looked round, and I followed her like I always did.

Above us, unexpected clouds covered the sun.

AT THE BAR, I BOUGHT A JD AND COKE FOR HER AND A PINT OF Guinness for me, then went to where she sat in a dark corner of the pub. Hard rock music pumped out just like we used to enjoy. The place was full of punks, rockers and burned out hippies. She gazed at me, as if she couldn't believe we were together again. Her eyes were as green as malachite, and she made me feel just like I used to; the mix of wanting her and wanting to please her, and all the time feeling as if she were mocking me. She smelled the same as well, she must be attached to that scent. I don't know what it was: flowers and sunshine and musk. More memories conjured by the perfume.

I took two rapid sips of the dark beer and read a poster about upcoming live bands.

"You look well," she said.

I gave a small laugh. "I'm working. I get exercise, eat well, don't do drugs."

"Joined the rat race, eh?" A gentle joke.

"Just got a better spin on things now."

She played with a silver ring on her finger, turning it round and round. It had three sprays, each of which held a differently coloured gemstone; emerald, ruby and sapphire. Simon bought her that, I remembered.

She said, "Simon was a shock to all of us. A wake up call, you know?"

I probably still loved her. Always had of course, and seeing her again, and smelling the mix of scent and skin took me back. We thought we were special, young and arrogant, like we were gods. The memory of our hubris made me almost sick now.

I said, "So where did you go?"

"Greece."

"You're not tanned."

She shook her head. "Everybody says that."

"Sorry."

She sipped her JD and coke and regarded me over the rim of her glass. "I worked in a library."

Not like her at all. I said, "A library? Do you speak Greek?"

"I've learned a bit of Greek."

I said, "Greece and Rome were Simon's things. Even when we were boys at home he loved his Greek Myths."

"Maybe that's why I went," she said quietly. Then, "What about you?"

"I work in a coffee shop. In Hampstead. Can't afford to live there though."

"In the coffee shop?"

"No, in Hampstead," I laughed. She could still make me laugh. "Or in the coffee shop either. It's a hipster joint and overpriced."

Janie Jones by the Clash came on. It made us talk about our band with Simon, though we both avoided saying his name, just like it was some kind of magic phrase, the uttering of which might work as a spell. We didn't mention him, but anyone listening would have sensed gaps in the story, like when someone burns out a face from a photograph with a cigarette.

We talked music. She laughed. I laughed. The band hadn't lived up to the promise of Simon's talent and Sofia's beauty because we were always too wasted on drugs to rehearse or look for gigs. But music was a love we had shared, me, her and the hole in the photograph.

Into the third pint, I said, "I never thought you'd come back, Sof."

Without looking up, she said, "Wasn't sure you ever wanted me to."

I never wanted her to know how much I had.

Her green eyes filled with tears. "I'll never forgive myself," she said.

The remains of dark bubbles huddled in the bottom of my glass.

She said, "You remember that time after the party on Primrose Hill."

I lied."No."

"Sure you do. We made the vow. We must have been on some mythological kick that day."

I shrugged. "Simon was."

She kept talking. "Remember, we vowed by the Furies? I didn't even know what they were then. Do now. You learn things like that in Greece."

I nodded. "Ah, yes, the Furies." I thought if I acknowledged it, she might shut up.

"And then we broke the vow," she said.

"It was all drunken bullshit."

"We said we'd look out for each other." Her smile was earnest, seeking something from me. I grunted and turned my attention from beer to ceiling.

"I admit it was my idea," she said. "Putting him on the road."

I exhaled. "I don't really want to talk about it."

She kept on. "You were right. If we'd called the ambulance at the beginning, he might have survived. I was just so scared of the police finding him in the flat and us all going to prison."

She looked like she might die there and then. Her mascara ran down her cheeks and she did nothing to wipe it away.

Compassion for our young stupid selves and the errors we'd made and compounded filled me. I put the back of my hand to her cheek. I said, "It was a long time ago."

She got out a handkerchief and wiped her eyes. "Look at me," she said, "What a mess." She laughed.

I took the hand away and gulped the last of my beer. "I should be going."

Then she took my hand again, pulled it to her and held it with both of hers. "Come to the flat with me?" she said.

I shook my head. "I don't think that's a good idea."

Her fingers were cold between mine. "I'm lost," she said. "I'm lost and I just need a friend."

I was pretty sure that friend wasn't me.

BACK AT THE FLAT IN CHALK FARM. WE SAT TOGETHER ON THE sofa. Initially, I'd sat on the chair, but she pulled me over. She sat close. I felt the warm skin of her arms against mine. She was talking about old friends and good times and pouring me then her a glass of wine. It was Greek wine, heavy as the sea —I thought of hemlock, given to those who remember but want to forget. My mind was wandering and strange. I felt the muscles and bones in her arm. Her hair draped across my shoulder. I leaned my head towards her. She smelled now of rose and jasmine.

"I put acid in your wine, Luke."

Just the sort of stupid trick she always used to play. She hadn't changed. "What?" I struggled to know what she meant. I wished I could wake from the waves that dragged me down.

"LSD, not battery." She giggled.

I went to stand. The walls whirred. Angels sang in birdlike chimes.

She took my wrist. "We always took it. You and me, while Simon took his heroin."

So this is what this was, some nostalgia trip.

She said, more thoughtfully this time. "I thought it would reset us. Reset our grief."

I shook my hand free of her grip. I said "What have you done? I don't want to get back into this."

"Just this once. Just you and me. Let's go on a trip together."

And the colours started to run. And the paintings in their frames on the apartment walls blurred and dripped and she sat close to me and I let the acid take me on its magic carpet ride. We laughed at how our faces melted. Just like they used to when I could forget I wasn't Simon.

. . .

IT WAS 10 AM WHEN I WOKE. TEN HOURS AFTER SHE GAVE ME THE acid the effects had mostly gone, but I was suffering the cracked out feeling the comes with the end of the trip. I stirred, shoved back the sheet with my arm, took a breath and rolled out of bed. Sofia groaned when I moved, but she slept on. The sheets were ruffled around her. Her hair was in her eyes and her mouth framed words as she conversed with dream lovers.

I rubbed my eyes. What had we done? In a panic, I had to get up. I pulled my pants on, then my shirt, and looked back at her. I had once wanted her so much that I had even wished my brother gone so I could have her. And now, this felt like Simon's final betrayal.

I let myself out quietly so as not to wake her, then walked home through the Sunday streets. It was really early. Maybe 5 a.m. There was no one about. It all went through my mind as I walked.

That long ago morning, we had vowed by the Furies that we would look after each other, but we still put a dying Simon on the road in the hope an ambulance would come and pick him up. We didn't know for sure he was dying, but we absolutely feared it. And yet, we didn't call the ambulance from the flat because we were drugged up and didn't want to get arrested. What a pair of shits. What a pair of unforgivable and unforgiven shits.

I walked the way home. All was normal until the phone rang in the phone box as I walked past it. That was the phone box that night. Now, it was one of the few remaining London red phone boxes. I stopped stock still. There was no one there, but still the phone in the phone box rang. At 5 a.m. I wanted to ignore it but I couldn't. I had the weirdest idea it was a message for me.

I turned and listened to the harsh bell ascend, repeat, lull, then repeat. Seconds strung to minutes, measured in fixed lengths of hammering bell. I ran my hand through my hair. I should just walk on. It meant nothing. It was just the after effects of the LSD making me think everything was significant. Sweat beaded on my brow and the ringing phone wound me up like a clockwork toy. I wanted to walk but the phone kept ringing. I stopped, stood and, slowly, turned. I would answer the phone just to prove it was a wrong number.

The black phone buzzed on its cradle inside the phone box. I saw it through the greasy glass just feet away. I stood and watched it ring, reaching out and feeling the vibration with my fingertips on the glass pane. I willed it to stop ringing. An insane iron bee that wouldn't stop.

It wasn't for me. With a grunt, I jerked the door open. I stepped in and I let the heavy door close behind me with a wheeze. The phone continued — insistent as an iron bee. I grabbed the receiver and I pressed it to my ear. "Who is it?"

A distant voice that sounded like it was echoing across shipless oceans said, "Luke?"

It was Simon's voice. I pressed my hand to my head. My mouth was dry. My heart raced.

"Luke?" he said again.

I slammed the phone down.

BY THE TIME I GOT TO MY FLAT, I STILL DIDN'T KNOW WHAT TO make of the voice. Reason told me it was a coincidence Luke was a common enough name. Just a wrong number and then a weirdness on top of it that made the person who answered be called Luke. But it had sounded like Simon's voice. I was trembling.

I unlocked the front door and stepped into the shared hallway, pushed my foot through the piles of junk mail addressed to people who no longer lived there and went upstairs to my flat. I had the key in my lock when I heard a growl behind me.

The hairs on my neck stood up and my heart started up again. I spun round and saw that halfway down the stairs from above was a black dog, its teeth bared. I'd seen one like it once before, but never here. I didn't know Tim — the guy upstairs — even had a dog and what was such an aggressive animal doing free in the communal areas?

I turned and scrabbled with the key and I pushed my way into the flat, slamming the door and heaving my back against it to make sure the dog couldn't come in.

I'm not afraid of dogs normally, but this one was like the devil himself. Door safely locked, I stood in the middle of the room and shook.

The flat was quiet and smelled of old cooking and me. I was exhausted emotionally after being with Sofia. It was still very early. I lay on the sofa and I remembered.

Like she said, Sofia and I took LSD, but Simon liked his heroin. Many times, I told him it would kill him, but he laughed and said he could control it. That night he fell asleep; more asleep than sleep itself. I didn't see his breathing slow down because I was fascinated by some glass beads Sofia had in a bowl. I was looking at them and laughing because my hand went transparent as I held them. I didn't hear Simon's breathing stop because I was looking at the whorls in the plaster ceiling that turned and spun like little fondant whirlwinds. It was Sofia who told me he was breathing dangerously shallowly.

I went to help him. I touched him with my fingers ends. He was still breathing but his skin was cooler than he should have been — warmer than the surroundings but colder than life. That temperature is a very awful thing, but I was in no state to deal with the ramifications of the situation because the colours kept colouring and the shapes kept shaping. The Acid wouldn't get out of my head just because my brother had overdosed.

I muttered, "We need to call an ambulance."

Sofia broke down in tears. "If they find him here, they'll arrest us all for drugs. My parents will kill me. He mustn't be found here."

I remembered the Furies. I said, "We promised to look after each other."

Sofia said, "Yes, he needs to go to hospital. But we need to get him outside and then we can call an ambulance."

It seemed to make sense. I lifted him, but he was heavy. Together we shifted him down the stairs. He bumped as we went down. His arm flopped. His head lolled and he made a sound. "He's alive," I said.

She nodded frantically. "Get him out quick then ring the ambulance. They'll save him."

I tried to keep him off the ground, but he was sliding down the stairs, making noises. Sofia opened the door and the whole still world was revealed. It was night and somewhere a police car sounded, but these streets were quiet. Not even a cat prowled. The night air was cool. We struggled with Simon and with an arm and leg each we heaved him down the street.

"Someone will see us," I said.

"Be quiet." Her forehead glistened with sweat. And we took him round the corner and I made to put him down.

"No! Not here." she hissed. "Too close."

We panted and laboured and got him further by a bush. "I can't carry him much further," I said. "And we need to get an ambulance, quick"

"Okay, okay. By this bush. But not covered," she said. "We want them to find him. He needs help."

He sure did. I laid him down carefully. I even brushed the slick hair out of his eyes.

"Come on," she said, dragging me by the hand. We ran back towards her flat. A light had come on upstairs from her neighbour's apartment on the upper floor. I glanced up. The window was open. An evil tempered black dog stuck its head out of a neighbour's window, watching us.

"We need to ring for the ambulance," I stammered.

"We can't ring from our place. They'll trace it," she said.

I said, "There's a phone box round the corner," , feeling like it was a brain-wave. Then a rainbow burst out from the clouds and the Acid played again.

She nodded. "Go." And I ran to the red phone box round the corner and I rang the ambulance from there, trying to disguise my voice, not giving my name.

That was five years ago. He died and we got away with it.

Only the dog saw. I didn't see Sofia afterwards. She said best not be in contact.

And then she was gone. To Greece, as it turned out.

Then I fell asleep.

· · ·

WHEN I WOKE IN MY FLAT, EVERYTHING WAS BACK TO NORMAL. Pale morning light displayed the worn carpet at its worst. I went to the front door. And then, out of habit, I turned over the piles of mail that lay on the rough-haired welcome mat. There was a letter face down. It looked odd, old somehow. The paper was yellowed. I leaned over and flipped it over. It had a stamp on it of a type I recognised from years ago. My name was handwritten on it in blue ink. I recognised the writing instantly. It was Simon's handwriting. I reeled back. Then I noticed another thing — the address was wrong. It was addressed to the place I'd lived years ago, at the time Simon died. Not here. Lots of explanations ran through my mind, but none of them convincing. I snatched the letter and ripped it open. Then, before pulling the paper from the envelope, I turned it and read the postmark. It was postmarked London NW1 and dated the day Simon died. I took the paper out with trembling fingers. I could hardly hold it straight. There was one sheet. I folded it open and saw that it was blank. Just old yellow paper. Nothing on it.

It crossed my mind I should ring Sofia after our night together. But I didn't.

ON MONDAY, I WENT TO WORK AT THE COFFEE SHOP. DURING MY lunch time in Hampstead, I passed by an alternative shop when a poster caught my eye. There was a workshop on the Greek goddesses of vengeance — the three Furies. That was a coincidence. I stopped and stared. There was a picture of them on the poster. One looked like Sofia, pale skin and black hair — the middle one. She was called Alekto.

I stepped into the shop, the bell on the door ringing wildly. A woman dressed all in white looked up from behind the counter.

"Hi," I said.

"Can I help?" she said mildly.

I jabbed my finger towards the poster in the window. "The Furies," I said. "There's a workshop?"

She nodded and said, "Next Tuesday. Entry £7.50 in the Assembly Rooms."

"Tell me about them," I said.

"Well," she shrugged. "Come to the workshop."

" Just tell me."

She frowned. "They were Greek goddesses of revenge. They were chthonic deities."

"What?"

"It means they were from under the earth. People sacrificed blood and flesh to them."

"What was their function?"

Her brow furrowed more deeply. "Their function was to hunt oath breakers."

"Oath-breakers."

"Yes, you know what that means?"

"Yes, of course." I hurried out of the shop, setting the bell ringing again.

"You're welcome," she called after me.

AT HOME LATER, I GOOGLED THE FURIES. I READ HOW THE KINDLY Ones emerged from the drops of Kronos' blood when it fell to earth, how they hunted those who broke their vows and how, the chief of them, Alekto, took the form of a black dog or a hooded maiden. They said there was no escape from her; her justice was inevitable.

That night walking back from work, I swear a dark-hooded woman followed me home. I walked fast, and then when I was in sight of my house, I ran. When I was in my kitchen, I looked out onto the road. There was no doubt that a woman, wearing a hood stood outside, watching me. I got it into my head that it was Alekto

I downloaded books on the Furies onto my Kindle, trying to see if there was a way an oath-breaker could escape their justice. Either pay them something or cheat them. I read more about the three of them; Nemesis revenged crimes against the gods, but Alekto revenged crimes on other humans, particularly the breaking of oaths. Black dogs accompanied her, those and black beetles.

The coincidences scared me: the call to the phone box I'd used that night. The horrible black dog on the landing that was identical with the one who watched us carry Simon that night.

I sat up late, frightened to sleep, watching Netflix on my phone, waiting for dawn. But even on those summer nights there were hours of darkness. Darkness kept at bay by electric lights. Finally, I grew so tired I slept on the couch.

And then someone knocked on my door. I woke from a dream and sat up. It was the middle of the night. I was in the living room. The door led directly to the hall outside. They were standing outside my flat in the communal area but they hadn't turned the light on.

I stopped breathing. The knock came again. I looked at the window. I thought I could jump out. The knock came again, gentle. Maybe it was Tim from upstairs who'd somehow got a black snarling dog. But what time was this to be knocking? I looked at my watch. Three a.m. My heart went cold. Three o'clock was the time Simon had died.

Another coincidence.

I cleared my throat. "Who is it?"

Silence.

I coughed. "Is there someone there?" I heard the floorboards outside move. Someone wanted to speak to me.

"Tim?"

No answer. The floorboards creaked again. Whoever it was, was still there.

My throat was tight and I was drenched in sweat. I jumped up and and flicked the room light on. It didn't make things better. The colours were drained by the harsh electric light. "If you're there Tim, can you answer?"

Tim didn't answer.

I sat on the bed, knees up, staring at the door. He was still there. I could sense it.

"Simon?" I said finally.

It was like he was waiting for me to open the door to him. I put my hand on the door handle. I turned the key. I just had to open the door and he would come in.

"Luke," he said from the other side of the door. "We need to talk."

"Go away, please, Simon. You're dead. Please go away."

There was a pause of a few seconds, then I heard him turn and leave.

I DIDN'T GO TO WORK THE NEXT DAY. I JUST SAT IN MY ROOM WITH the door locked. I heard my neighbour Tim go out and come in and then go out again. I was in a hell of a state. I thought I should go out and maybe get some alcohol. Maybe something stronger. But I wasn't even able to do that. I couldn't move from my room. The night drew on. Darkness fell. I watched TV. Then I couldn't concentrate. I switched the TV off and sat there listening to cars pass outside, until they finally quietened. I had the lamp on beside my bed.

I heard a noise outside. I swallowed hard. If this was Simon. I would speak to him. He'd tried to contact me three times. Strange and terrible as it was, he must need to speak to me.

But then I heard the growl of a dog. I pushed myself back in the couch. It wasn't Simon. I heard a low chanting – ritual words in a foreign tongue.

The electric light flickered. I heard a buzzing in the air. The dog growled louder. It was just outside the door. I wouldn't unlock it. I couldn't unlock it. I was petrified: turned to stone through fear of what was coming.

But she didn't need me to unlock the door.

The lamp failed and she came. The vermin came first, or rather the pre-shadowing of them. I heard the scuttling of beetles and in what light there was, saw them all over the floor. I shrieked and jumped on the bed while they pitter-pattered beneath it and mounted the walls. I had my phone, which still had battery, though no signal. It gave a weak light and I could see them, exotic and out of place, shell backed and black carapace.

Then the dog appeared: a savage black dog, teeth bared, snarling. The same dog that saw me the night I killed Simon.

The chanting grew louder. I guessed now it was in Ancient Greek. Ritual words of some ancient retribution.

I couldn't see her at first. Her voice came from the walls and the air.

She spoke my name, and even the beetles listened. The dog went quiet, while its mistress spoke. "Luke," she said.

I clutched my knees to my chest. I thought my heart would jump from my throat. My palms were soaked. I couldn't swallow the spit that flooded my mouth for fear I would choke.

"Luke," she said again. This time her voice was close. She whispered my name in my ear as if to make sure she had the right person.

I jerked away, almost falling from the couch. "Go away," I cried.

She coalesced into the room. In the wavering coloured light of my phone I saw her come fully into being. At first she was a shower of particles, like a black dust, but these particles then took life and moved, forming her limbs, and her torso. Finally, I saw Alekto, black haired and black robed. I recognised her from descriptions I'd read. At first I thought it was hair, but then saw the sinuous bodies of serpents, black scaled, darting tongues, writhing around her like a dark halo. The serpents grew from her and twined in her hair and down her shoulders.

And when she opened her white iris-less eyes, blood dripped from them onto her white cheeks like tears.

These were not the salt tears of mercy, they were the scarlet tears of vengeance.

I begged her to forgive me for breaking my oath to Simon, but the powers of the old earth care not for the softness of men; they care only for the punishment of those who break their oaths. We had sworn an oath by the old powers. Not to punish me was to allow mockery of the gods themselves, and the pride of gods will not allow mockery. The Furies will not allow their names to be taken in vain.

She stood watching me, crying her tears of blood, her mouth half open, her teeth those of a snake. I bolted, landing with my feet on the floor, crushing beetles underfoot as I yanked at the door with shaking hand. I ran to the front door. It would be locked, but I had the key in my jeans. I hadn't undressed so I still had it on me.

I jumped down the communal stairs, and then I was in the hall. The front door let in streetlight. That was my escape route.

But something stood in my way. There, in the room, was the dog. It stood, snarling in the gloom, blocking my escape. I spun round in a panic. It was before me, she behind. I turned and saw her descending the stairs towards me. Even without lights, she gave off her own dark luminosity, the snakes in her hair hissing and twisting, her mouth open to show her lamprey maw. Her hands were out in supplication, their claws pearlescent against the skin of her white fingers.

She said, "Your brother wanted to forgive you. But I will not tolerate that."

❧ 7 ☙

THE FROG GOD

Autumn's coming. I can see the leaves turning, catching yellow in the mellow sunlight. A breeze blows off the Thames but the sun's still warm. It's Sunday afternoon in Greenwich and we're in the central market area with all its stalls and crafts and bric a brac. I smell chilli dogs and French fries from the San Antonio Street Food stall and hummus with falafel from the Syrians. All good.

I'm with Melissa. Melissa isn't my girlfriend though that would be kind of nice. Melissa is my landlady. She inherited a house in Greenwich so let me come to live there for a nominal rent. I couldn't afford to be round here otherwise. We met through a website called Gig-Mates because we share an interest in electronic music, Ghost Box and the Heartwood Institute and stuff like that.

Melissa is pretty. Her father's Japanese and her mother's English. She has long dark hair and a face like a doll. Her boyfriend is equally attractive, and rich, and clever, and really nice.

As we walk, Melissa's attention is caught by a particular stall where a man with a leather hat and twinkling brown eyes is trying to sell a print of the coronation of King George V to an old lady.

'Hey, I like that vase!' Melissa points. It's tall. It's got flowers on it. Blue ones I think. I shrug.

She goes up, the old lady moves on King George still unbought and he latches onto Melissa. They talk about the jug, but my eye is caught by a jade statuette of a frog. It looks Chinese. It's only about three inches high, and it's stuck right out at the front of the stall, like he didn't want to infect all the other bits of junk. Except this doesn't look like junk. I pick it up and turn it over in my hand. It's heavy, smooth and warm. It feels like jade. He only wants a quid for it. Looks like a bargain. Then I get a weird sensation from the statuette, like I've just dipped my fingers in cold oil, tingly and smeary. I put the frog down, then I examine my fingers but there's nothing smeared on them. It was a weird sensation though. Melissa's still talking to the geezer in the leather hat.

I narrow my eyes and stare. That frog must be worth more than a pound. It looks like an antique. I get my phone and photograph it. I half-worry that the stall owner will object to me taking a photo, but he's still talking to Melissa, his good sense undermined by her good looks. She gets that a lot. But then, just for an instant, I swear he glanced in my direction and clocked what I was doing, and then I think it's like he is deliberately ignoring my interest in his little frog thing, but I dismiss that as stupid. Why would he do that?

A quick image search on the internet throws up similar images. Some aren't so similar but a couple are.

One is actually strikingly similar. It's almost a duplicate. The website about Chinese Jade Carvings says it is made from Xiuyan Jade from Northeastern China. The one in the picture that looks just like the one on the stall dates from the Han Dynasty and is of the frog god *qīng wā shén*. Apparently he exists to punish thieves. Amazing what you learn from the Internet.

More amazing is that the frog god statuette I've just looked up sold for over half a million pounds two years ago. I breathe in hard. I didn't mean to. Greed goes off like the fruit machine reels and they come up five cherries in a row. He only wants a quid?

Melissa is finished talking to him now. She didn't buy the vase, but he takes that well. He's just grinning at her. I clear my throat. 'Mate?'

The man walks off. He goes to talk to his pal on the stall behind that sells railway models. I raise my voice. 'Mate?' He doesn't turn. I look at the frog. I could just take it. It's right at the front of the table.

Melissa asks, 'What are you after?'

I point. 'The jade frog.'

'It's horrible,' she says. 'A nasty little piece.'

I whisper, 'It's an antique. I think.'

She lifts it, turns it over. It's got a makers mark on the bottom: a Chinese character. It looks old. 'Eww,' she says, putting it down in a hurry. 'It feels nasty and oily.'

'Mate?' I say, but he still doesn't turn.

Melissa catches my elbow. 'Come on. I'm hungry. Fancy some falafel?'

I sigh. It doesn't look like he's heard me. He only wants a quid for it. She's tugging at me. 'Excuse me!' I yell. He's deep in conversation with the railway modeller. He's deliberately ignoring me. It's rude. It's almost as if he wants me to steal the frog.

'Come on, Sam,' Melissa says. 'He obviously doesn't need the sale.'

I look at it. Half a million quid. He's not interested in selling it to me. I could just snatch it and leave the pound on the table.

I shout, 'A pound, is it? This frog?' He doesn't turn. I put my hand in my jeans and pull out a pound coin. I slap the coin on the table, grab the frog and stuff it into my coat pocket. 'Thank you. There's a quid on the table.'

Melissa drags me off. 'Or a chilli dog or hummus?' she says.

'Melissa,' I say, my heart hammering. 'I think this frog's worth half a million quid.'

She laughs. She doesn't believe me. She says, 'Get you, Mr Bargain Hunter! Worth half a million and you get it for a pound! What a steal!'

LATER THAT DAY, ABOUT 7 PM, MELISSA ANNOUNCES SHE IS GOING TO her boyfriend's.

'Are you?'

'Yes, I told you We're going to see his parents in Harrogate. I'll be away all week.'

'Did you say?'

'Yes, Sam. Really, you never pay attention!' She's smiling as she says it. I work 12 hour shifts as a hospital porter – I said I couldn't afford to live in Greenwich at market rate rents. That means I get four days off a week. Today was my first day off. Looked like I'd be alone in the house for the next three days.

She leaves and I go for a pint at the Cutty Sark. I know them in there. I just have two beers and read my book, then I go home.

Our place is down a small cul-de-sac. It's not modern. The house probably dates from the early 1800s, but the street is quiet outside with an old fashioned single sodium lamp giving out yellow light. The house is in darkness as I turn my key in the lock. The first thing I notice is the smell. It smells like the river's got in — really damp. I switch on all the lights and go looking for a leak, but the radiators are all okay. The boiler pressure is okay. I even venture down into the cellar to see if the water table has risen up, but there's no sign of water anywhere. Still, it smells like a swamp.

I light a joss-stick to drive the stink away, and sit down in the front room with its old comfortable leather sofa and chairs and bookshelves then I switch on the modern TV and watch a programme about the Knights Templar, then one about Ancient Aliens. After a couple of hours, I go to bed. The jade frog is on the top of my chest of drawers. It looks innocuous enough, but there's something about it I don't like. As I take my clothes off and pull on my pyjamas, I tell it, 'You are going to make my fortune, good boy.'

I have a plan to get it valued by Christie's or Sotheby's. I'll do that tomorrow. Then I sleep.

I wake up shivering. The room is really cold. The swamp smell is stronger now. I have the weird feeling that there's something in the room with me. I tell myself not to be stupid. It's just because I'm not used to being alone in the old house. I haven't drawn the curtains properly so light from the lamp outside slants in yellow and catches the jade frog. It just sits there quietly.

I look back at the window. I just can't shake off the feeling of a presence. I think maybe I heard something outside and that's what woke me. I throw back the duvet and slip out of the bed, stepping to the window and peering out through the gap in the curtains.

I see nothing outside. Just darkness and shadows. It's started to rain slightly. I see nothing but I still feel there's something there, lurking out of sight. I always was prone to irrational imaginings. This is another. I shake my head and turn back to bed.

I catch the frog out of the corner of my eye. It seems like it's watching me.

Of course it can't be watching me; it's made of jade. It has no intelligence. As I sink into bed and pull up the duvet, I steal a glance at it. It's inscrutable, watching me out of its carved eyes. Then I think that it's the frog god who punishes thieves. Except I didn't steal the frog. I paid for it fair and square. He only wanted a pound and a pound is what I gave him. Not my fault if he didn't know the true value.

I don't sleep at all. I just lie there imagining the frog staring at me. I'm glad when morning light spills into the room. The frog's still there. I ignore it and go downstairs. When Sotheby's opens, I'm on the phone. Instead of brushing me off, the bloke sounds interested. I send him a photo of the Chinese character on the bottom and he's very interested. 'I think you've got the real thing there, Sam. Can you bring it in?'

I say I can, but I don't rush. I want to make them wait for it. I don't want them to think I'm an easy touch. I want its full value. I say I'll take it in tomorrow.

Another night, another trip to the Cutty Sark, more TV when I get home, except I can't settle. I keep thinking of the jade frog upstairs. When I get to bed, I put it in the sock drawer out of sight, but when I wake in the middle of the light, by the gleam of the sodium lamp outside, I see the frog is back on the top of the chest of drawers where it was before I hid it.

The stink of swamp water is incredible. But worse than that — I hear the noise of something breathing. Something damp and old and huge. Last night it was outside, now it's in the house. I put the frog back in the drawer, lock the drawer and for good measure, listen by my door to the sound of whatever has entered the house. I feel it. I hear it. I smell it. Whatever's downstairs has come for me. I lock the bedroom door.

I don't remember sleeping. I check the room all the time. But by morning, the frog is back on the top of the chest of drawers, escaped from the locked drawer. Quietly watching me. Waiting.

The next day, I don't take the frog to Sotheby's I take it back to Greenwich Market. I want shot of it. The bric a brac man with the leather hat is gone. I ask the Railway Modeller man next door where he went.

'He's having a break, mate. Won't be here for a while.'

'Has he gone away?'

'Why do you want to know?'

'Just...' I don't know how to say this. 'Just I...'

'Yeah?'

'I stole something from him.'

'Stole something from him? And now you've got an attack of conscience. Should I call the coppers?'

I shake my head. 'Well, not stole, but I got it for a fraction of what it's worth. It's really valuable. He didn't know.'

The railway modeller laughs. 'I doubt that, mate. Georgios knows his antiques. If it was worth something, he would know.'

'I need to give him it back.'

'Because it's worth more than he thought?'

'Yes.'

'Well, that's decent of you, mate, but that's business. Not many as honest as you.'

'Does he live nearby?'

'I can't tell you that.'

'Please, I want to give it back to him.' Then I think. 'Or you could?' I take the frog out of my pocket. I thrust it at him but he recoils, hands up. 'Oh, that! He hated that thing.'

I stop. 'Why did he hate it?'

'He never said. I don't think he'll want it back though.'

'Please, I don't want to rip him off. Just tell me where he lives?'

'I can't tell you, mate. Sorry.'

So I go to walk off, then I see a chipped sign on the empty table where Giorgios had his stall. It says, 'Attica Antiques; Proprietor G. Kritikos.'

A bit of googling later and a check in an online phone book and I have his address. More than one G Kritikos, but only one in Greenwich. It's not far. I hurry round, the leaves heaped on street corners, rubbish in the gutters, dirty shops with dirty shutters and then a row of residential houses just back from the main road. I recognise him as soon as he answers the door. From the look on his face, he recognises me too, which is significant.

I thrust the frog towards him, but he steps back. 'I don't want that,' he says raising both hands as if afraid to touch it. 'You keep it. You bought it fair and square.'

'You know it's worth a fortune?' I say.

He just stares at me hard-faced. 'You bought it fair and square.'

'I didn't. I embezzled you.'

'Not really.'

'It wasn't a fair exchange.'

'I'm fine, mate. It's yours.'

I pause. 'There's something wrong with it.'

He doesn't laugh. He doesn't call me crazy, he just tries to shut the door on me. I put my foot against the door, so he can't push it closed.

'Hey,' he says, 'I'll call the police.'

That's an idea. I say, 'Call the police. I'll admit to stealing to from you. They'll take it off me.'

'No, you bought it.'

'At such a price, it was wrong. It was like theft.'

He narrows his eyes. 'You know in Chinese law, theft isn't just plain stealing. Theft also includes fraud and embezzlement and plain old cheating. I got that from an old bloke in a house clearance. His son got it in China and then died he told me. He was selling up because he had to pay for his care. I paid him pennies for it. I knew it was valuable. I was greedy just like you. But it's yours now, mate. You knew what it was worth, and you paid far less, criminally less, so by Chinese rules, you stole it.'

With that I withdraw my foot and he slams the door.

My mind is racing as I go home. I guess the old bloke didn't get punished because he inherited it rather than stole it. Sounded like his son got it by sharp practice though.

About 2 am, exhausted, I fall asleep, the frog locked away.

A noise awakes me. The house is cold. It feels damp. My bedroom door is open though I'm sure I locked it. I glance at the chest of drawers. The jade frog isn't there. It must be in the drawer where I put it, but when I look, that drawer is open and the frog is gone.

The house is damp and cold, but I'm hot; burning up like I have a fever. I wonder if I've got a bug. I go to the bathroom and take some paracetamol. Then I think maybe the shower would cool me down. I set the water temperature to lukewarm, strip off and step in. Our shower is in the bath, so I stand there, behind the shower curtain with the water playing on my head and shoulders. It doesn't really help, makes it worse. I'm about to get out when I hear croaking outside the bathroom. The croaking of a hundred frogs. I hear them moving. Their life cold and alien outside the shower curtain. Then I hear a wet flop, then another, as hundreds of squirming frogs hop and jump into the shower.

I scream for help but Melissa is away, and if the neighbours hear me, they ignore it, like we all ignore things in London. I look at the floor. It's covered with squirming green and yellow of all different sizes. The frogs hop up onto and into the bath. I feel them cold and damp as they jump up against my thighs and hips. I press myself backwards and slip on the wet bath. I go down, they're going to bury me in their foul bony bodies. First one, then another, then another until the weight of twenty or thirty or forty frogs is on me. They jump onto my face and I feel their cold feet and see their eyes in the bathroom light. They are drowning me − cold moving bags of hard bones. I scream again and jump up, scattering them. Wherever, they've touched me I have burns from the slime that covers their damp, soft skin. They're burning me. Hopping at me. I run out of the bathroom, squelching them underfoot and where their cold bodies squash, going between my bare toes, they scald me.

At least, I have the foresight to grab my trousers and shirt and coat as I run out of the door, leaving it open.

. . .

THE NURSE PRACTITIONER AT ACCIDENT AND EMERGENCY HAS never seen anything like it. 'Like alkaline burns. Lots of them. What've you been up to? And how come you've got no shoes?'

I don't tell her. How could I? She treats the wounds, dresses them, and gives me some pain-killers. I get a taxi back. The driver doesn't speak. By the time I get to the house, it's day. The front door is wide open. It's a wonder we've not been burgled. There are the mashed bodies of green and yellow frogs here and there where I stepped on them, but otherwise no sign of the cold plague that hopped and jumped all over me.

God knows what will happen to me if I stay there tonight. I could run, but I have the feeling the frog god will find me wherever I go.

The jade frog sits on top of the chest of drawers, watching me. I dress cautiously. I'm in agony from my wounds. I snatch it, and put it into my pocket. Then I head out.

It's 09:30. I go to the first builders café I see. It's full of men in high-vis jackets having mugs of tea with bacon butties or Full English breakfasts. They're working on the construction sites. I hear Irish accents, a Geordie, some Jamaicans and then Cockneys.

I order a mug of tea with a bacon sandwich. When it comes, I bite into it and the melted butter drips on my chin. The bacon is crisp, the bread soft. I didn't realise how hungry I was. Surreptitiously I take the jade frog from my pocket and put it on the formica topped table. It takes me ten minutes to finish the sandwich and the mug of tea. I stand up and step away. It feels good to leave that foul statuette behind. I get to the door when someone yells, 'Oi, mate, you've forgot your thing.'

A builder is coming up behind me. He has the frog in his hands. He tosses it to me. 'What is it, anyway? Ugly little bleeder. Feels greasy.'

I just grunt.

He says, 'You're welcome,' then turns back to his mates.

I find the Greenwich Tunnel and go down in the lift, the jade frog a hard lump in my coat pocket. My mind is spinning. I need to get someone to steal this off me. I walk and walk on the other side until I'm wandering the Isle of Dogs. This used to be a place of poor people. Surely someone will steal this thing from me here.

I see a group of school kids hanging round outside a newsagent. They are a rowdy, multi-racial gang and mouthy to the woman in the shop.

I sit on a bench. A couple of teenage girls, one black, one white make up thickly plastered to their faces, short skirts way above the knee; they look really rough. 'Got a fag, mate?'

'No.'

'Got any drugs?'

'No.'

'You're no fucking fun, are ya?'

I just nod. They dissolve in laughter. I get the frog and put it on the bench beside me. I don't look at it. I sit for ten minutes then get up, walk off, leaving it. I hope if they just take it it counts as theft. After all, I didn't give it to them.

I'm about a hundred yards away when I hear a call. 'Bruv? This is yours, innit? I fink you forgot it. Don't you like it? '

I half turn. 'I don't want it.' Then I'm gripped by panic. If I say that I'm giving it away then no one will take the guilt of my theft.

But I hear running feet. The black girl who wanted the cigarette thrusts the frog into my hand. I hardly want to accept it, but I do. She smiles sweetly. 'You nearly lost this. Thought it might have sentimental value.'

'Thank you,' I manage.

When the hell did people get so honest?

Later, I'm in Canary Wharf. It's mid-afternoon but some well dressed, suited financiers are well into their champagne at the wine bar. I go in. I try to order a beer. The bar steward looks down his nose at me and says, 'We don't serve beer here, sir.'

'Give me a whiskey and soda then. Make it a double.'

It cost me £12. I sit. I brood on my drink, then I get another. I'm anticipating returning to the house. I can't bear it. I take the jade frog out and place it on the table where it sits looking at me. I watch the people go past, laughing. The table next to me are talking about yachts and holiday homes in France.

I get up to go to the toilet, leaving the frog on the table. As, I go past the table with the drunken bankers, I overhear one of them whisper, 'Hey, look at that. I bet that's worth something.'

I don't go back to the table. I head straight out the door.

I wait outside as darkness comes. I want to see them leave with it, not leave it behind. I need someone to steal it, so if it's left, I'll have to go and ask if it's been handed in.

I see them leave, really drunk now, expensive suits. The blokes give each other manly chest bumps in an ironic way and air kiss the lady bankers and part, each going separate ways.

I really don't know if they've got it. I'm going to have to go back in and ask the bartender if anyone's handed it in.

I almost get to the door of the bar, the bankers still saying their farewells. And then, one, a handsome blonde man splits off and heads off for his train down the concrete canyon between the towering sky scrapers. And as he goes, I see the shadow of a huge frog hop after him.

8

TICK TOCK

I t was the endless ticking that kept her awake though she couldn't work out where it was coming from. Typically, she would fall asleep and then wake to hear it. She didn't notice it during the day, though she wasn't in much during the day to be honest, but at night, it was like it got louder and louder after midnight then faded away after two-thirty a.m. Precisely two-thirty, Sarah Jones knew that because she checked it every damned night.

Sarah had a house and a husband and two children in Hertford-shire, but as an up-and-coming barrister with chambers in the Middle Temple she found she was spending a lot of time commuting and so took a new flat in Stepney to stay in during the week. It was small and would be an excellent investment. Her flat was part of a fresh develop-ment of some Fifties council flats that had been sold off and upcycled. Some developer had knocked the old buildings down and put up a condominium with a concierge and security and a car park below ground where she could park during the week saving her a fortune.

It was perfect. Perfect that is, apart from the ticking. Sarah asked the concierge to ask the handyman to fix it, but he couldn't come up with a solution. In fact, he claimed he couldn't even hear it.

Sarah said, 'Maybe it only happens at night.'

'Between midnight and two-thirty?' he said.

'Yes,' she said.

'Really,' he said. He sounded unconvinced in the way workmen have. But he couldn't fix it.

ONE SUNDAY SARAH STAYED IN LONDON. SHE HAD WORK TO DO AND Mike understood. But she gave herself a break too, and that gave her the opportunity to meet Elaine — an old University friend from Oxford. They'd lived together in digs in Cowley for a year. Elaine had read History while Sarah studied Law. Elaine worked now at the Museum of London at the Barbican. She didn't earn much, but she seemed happy. Sarah thought that was the most important thing: to be happy in your work.

They were walking past St Botolph's Church at Aldgate when the congregation filed out.

'That's a big congregation for Sunday in the City,' Sarah said.

'It's the Blitz commemoration service — for all the local Londoners who lost their lives in the Luftwaffe bombing in the Second World War.' Elaine knew these London historical things of course but she could be a bit snippy with it sometimes. Sarah arched her eyebrows. 'I know what the Blitz was, Elaine...'

Elaine blushed. 'Want a coffee? There's a Starbucks open down there.'

WORK WAS BUSY. THE DAYS WENT BY. WINTER DEEPENED AND IT was getting colder every day. She was so focused that Sarah didn't notice the ticking. The man must have fixed it, or maybe it just went away. She didn't notice it that is until halfway through January. It was bitter cold and dark and there were even flurries of snow. The world had its face turned from summer and it seemed to be night for almost twenty-four hours at a stretch. When the day did show its face, the sun hid behind clouds and it was dull and grey and went away quickly. Sometimes she walked to work along the Embankment and saw the Thames wreathed with mist and grey waves smelling of weed and oil and the muddy estuary lapped the banks at full tide.

THE SENSE OF SOMEONE ARRIVING SHOCKED SARAH AWAKE. IT WAS the middle of the night. Tuesday. And dark.

She'd been working late, had a glass of wine and crashed out. The wine glass, half-drunk, was beside her bed. Someone was there in the room, she knew it. And the ticking was back, tapping and clicking its way into her head. She pushed herself up against the headboard, and called in her strongest voice, 'Hello? Who's there?'

Silence: but an odd, echoing silence, as if something had been removed. Like antimatter, negative energy. It hung there, waiting.

'Hello?' Sarah said again. She was afraid. 'Just take what you want. Please don't hurt me.'

Darkness waited silently, more solid in the room's corner. Thick curtains were drawn at the window. She could hardly make anything out. The only light came from a red pinprick from her phone charger.

Then she saw what had come. The woman developed from the darkness like an old photograph in a dish of chemicals. She precipitated into the room. She was an ordinary-looking woman, pale, average height and weight. Light brown hair in a permanent wave. Her clothes looked old-fashioned. 1930s? 1950s? Sarah had trouble calibrating her usually excellent brain.

Sarah drew in a slow, raggedy breath. Goose bumps stood up on her bare arms. The spirit woman said nothing. And then she just faded out through the bedroom door.

'I've seen a ghost,' Sarah said to herself. 'I've never seen one before. I never believed in them. But that's what that was.'

Later, when she'd composed herself, she got up, switched all the lights on and looked around the flat. The door was locked and there was no sign of forced entry. No sign of anyone being there at all. It wasn't a burglar. It was a ghost.

· · ·

Over a glass of champagne in a City wine bar, Elaine narrowed her eyes. 'Really?' Elaine was as concrete as the Barbican. She'd always been like that. Skeptical. Sarah actually thought Elaine only ever believed in things she could personally lift. And, in fact, Sarah wasn't in the mood for these things to be explained away by Elaine. She said, 'Yes! I swear. It came with that damned ticking, and now I come to think of it, when she vanished the ticking went with her.'

Elaine had heard the ticking story many times. She still looked like she didn't believe it. 'So it was two-thirty in the morning?'

'I suppose so. It was something like that. The middle of the night.'

Elaine took a sip. 'I'm surprised you believe in that stuff. You're usually so level-headed'

Sarah had a Tarot pack in her twenties. The nice Aquarian one. There were lots of things Elaine didn't know about her. She sipped her Veuve Clicquot.'I don't need to believe in it. I saw it.'

Elaine did that thing with her eyebrow. 'Hmm.'

Sarah felt her irritation grow but determined not to show it. 'Really!' She was a barrister. How could Elaine think she would lie?

'And she vanished?'

'She sort of went through the door.'

'Did she open it?'

'No, she was kind of absorbed through it.'

'And she vanished then?'

Sarah shrugged. 'I don't know. She wasn't in the hall when I went out later.'

'Must've vanished then.'

'You don't believe me.'

'Well... Had you had your wine?'

'That has nothing to do with it.'

'Of course not.'

The next night the woman visited again; the grey-faced woman in her dowdy old-fashioned clothes. The ticking was loud;

exactly like an alarm clock. The spirit woman just stared at Sarah; she didn't speak.

Sarah sat, pushed up against the headboard, the duvet hugged to her. She wasn't as scared this time. 'Can you see me?' Sarah said. She wondered if the woman was lost in some netherworld neither seeing nor hearing, just fated to return to this place for eternity for who knows what purpose?

The woman still didn't speak, but there was something more urgent about her. Sarah was sure they could see each other.

'What do you want?' Sarah said, emphasising each word like she was talking to someone who didn't understand English properly.

The woman just went backwards through the door.

'Well,' Sarah said. 'How strange.'

She thought she'd just vanished like last time. Then the door clicked open. She was sure it had been securely closed, but it clicked open and now it swung ajar, about six inches, as if inviting her.

Sarah knew somehow the woman wanted her to follow. She got up, put on her thick dressing gown and padded bare-foot out of the bedroom. The parquet flooring was cool underfoot. And there the woman stood by the door to her flat. This door was definitely mortice locked; it wasn't just going to click open.

The woman vanished through the door backwards. She definitely wanted Sarah to follow.

Sarah unlocked the door with trembling hands and stepped out onto the communal landing. There was the lift, gleaming and silent, and the stairs. The woman was on the stairs.

Sarah later couldn't describe the woman's movement exactly. It was odd. She didn't walk and she didn't exactly float; she just somehow moved. And she moved downstairs.

Sarah followed, trembling not with cold, but with a mix of fear and excitement. The woman went down the next flight and from here the stairs led below to the carpark.

'What do you want?' Sarah hissed at the ghost that stood sad and expectant, waiting for Sarah to follow her into the basement.

There was a noise behind her. 'Are you all right?' A man's voice spoke, making Sarah jump out of her skin. She turned and saw coming down the passage from the front door where the concierge's office was, the same handyman who had been sceptical about the ticking sound.

'What are you doing here?' Sarah said.

'I work here,' he said rather insolently.

Sarah said, 'I thought you were the handyman.'

'I'm doing extra. Bill's off sick, so I'm covering his night shift.'

Sarah glanced back to the stairs. The ghost had now gone. 'Did you see a woman?' she asked the man.

He grinned. 'You.'

A real smart Alec. Sarah huffed. 'No, another woman, going downstairs.'

'Into the car park?'

'Yes.'

He shook his head. 'You're the only woman I've seen for hours."

They stood silently for a while. He was mocking her. She hated that. She was a woman of authority, here she was being mocked by a janitor in his twenties.

Without speaking again, she went back upstairs to her flat and locked the door securely behind her. The ticking noise had stopped. It was quarter to three in the morning.

THE THIRD TIME THE WOMAN CAME, SARAH WAS WAITING FOR HER. It was 2 a.m. She appeared as she always did, like a grey angel, just materialising in the bedroom by the door.

'Hello,' Sarah said, as if it was all perfectly normal.

The woman said nothing, she just stepped backwards through the door and the door opened with a click. The clock noise tick-tocked through Sarah's head. It seemed it was coming from everywhere now, all around, insistent and loud as if it too had a message for her.

Sarah hurried down into the hallway. The ghost awaited her on the stairs down to the carpark. The janitor wasn't around. Sarah followed the ghost, down the steps, down onto the ground floor. The spirit woman went ahead down the dark steps to the basement care park. Sarah looked around. Still no sign of the handyman. She clicked on the light, half expecting the ghost to vanish in the brightness of electric light, but here at the bottom the ghost lingered. She was translucent, just like they say ghosts are supposed to be.

Pulling her dressing gown tight against the cold, Sarah went down in her bare feet. There was a door. Locked, but it had a keypad. The ghost went straight through it, and Sarah pressed in the numbers and followed.

They were in the basement car park now. Under street level. Sarah shivered from the cold. All around her gleaming, high-performance cars waited quietly like patient steel horses. It was silent, so silent, apart from the ticking of the clock, in her head and all around.

The ghost woman waited near the centre of the concrete floor. She waited for Sarah to take notice. Sarah didn't know what she was supposed to take notice of. The floor chilled the soles of Sarah's feet. The woman descended into the ground. She melted through the floor, disappearing, foot by knee by hip by chest until even her head was gone.

Sarah couldn't follow her underground.

But the tick-tocking, ticked and tocked, a metallic clicking inside her head, setting her teeth on edge.

That was the message. Dig down. There was something there.

The handyman was against it, but he wasn't the boss. In the end, Sarah had to say she'd pay if they found nothing. The owner of the building was actually intrigued; he believed in the supernatural and signs and, he'd got it into his head they were going to find a pot of Roman gold under the basement of his garage.

Elaine stood with her as the men with the pneumatic drill cut through the concrete. The noise was dreadful. The men had ear defenders, but Elaine and Sarah had to clap their hands over their ears instead.

'Bloody hell! What's that?'

The man stopped drilling.

Everyone all rushed over and stared at what they'd uncovered in the damp London clay, studded with broken bricks from former buildings, some blackened and burned. The man screamed at them to get back.

It wasn't Roman gold. It was an unexploded German bomb.

LATER, ELAINE EXPLAINED. 'I LOOKED UP YOUR ADDRESS. ON 9 September 1940, the Luftwaffe dropped tons and tons of bombs on this site.'

Sarah said, 'But one didn't go off.'

Elaine lifted a finger. 'That was on purpose. They would drop a stick of bombs and some of them were designed to bury themselves and had a timer so they blew up when they reckoned the rescue workers were there.'

Sarah said, 'Wicked. Did say that the army bomb disposal said it was about to go off? The fuse had rotted through and the timing mechanism was long gone, but it was in such a dangerous state that it would have blown the whole building to kingdom come.' She took a gulp of champagne. 'I'm just glad that woman came to warn us. I wonder who she was?'

Elaine said, 'I checked the records and it turned out that when the bombs blew up the buildings that were on your site they killed over twenty people. One was a woman called Sarah Jones.'

'Sarah Jones? That's my name.'

Elaine said, 'And dead Sarah came back to warn living Sarah the bomb was about to go off.'

Sarah said, 'So you believe me now?'

Elaine smiled. 'Sarah, dear, you were always histrionic, but never a liar. I always believed you.'

Sarah lifted an elegant eyebrow. 'Of course you did.'

❀   *9*   ❀

BAD TIMES IN LITTLE VENICE

'You're a lucky man,' Simon Wroxhall said smiling, and Sandip thought he was too. You could tell that from the enormous grin all over his face. Sandip was young, only twenty-five. He was bright too, bright as a button, just not very street wise.

Sandip just landed a top job at LonGen, a family-owned genetics research firm that had a lucrative contract for the National Health Service in developing gene therapy approaches to cancer and congenital disorders. The owner, Simon Wroxhall, built it up from scratch after his days at laboratories at Cambridge University. Now fantastically successful, LonGen was housed in the shell of an old Edwardian House in Maida Vale, near Westbourne Park tube and the Westway.

Feeling he had finally arrived, Sandip looked around him. LonGen's offices were discreet and plush. They looked antique and tasteful from the outside, but inside the house it was shiny and clean and modern; purpose-built to the highest specifications for a high tech, groundbreaking genetic research and therapy company.

Simon leaned in and tapped Sandip on the knee. 'But what got you the job wasn't your wonderful CV, it was your consuming curiosity.'

Sandip sat back, grinning ever more broadly. He didn't know if consuming curiosity was a good thing, but if it had got him the job, then why not? 'Thanks,' he said.

Simon went on, stroking his grey flecked black beard. 'We trawled through hundreds of candidates and your academic record is top notch, but you have the right personality too. It's important that our people fit in with who's already here.'

'Thank you, Mr Wroxhall,' Sandip said. 'It's a great privilege to work here. Such fantastic colleagues, and of course I'm very pleased with the salary. Very generous.'

Simon smiled. 'Sorry we didn't give you a car, but we've conscious of our impact on the environment.'

'That's okay,' Sandip said. 'I've got my bike.'

Later on, by the water cooler, Sandip stood with Walter. He hardly knew him, but he was so new, he hardly knew anyone at LonGen. 'Hey,' Sandip said.

'Hello,' replied Walter, filling up his bamboo cup. 'Enjoying the job?'

Sandip winced. 'Yeah, but it's always the same when you start a new job — bit confusing. Still learning the computer system. We had Radix at Cambridge.'

'Yeah, Radix is good, but I think Mesa is better.'

Sandip shrugged. 'I'll get to grips with it.'

Walter said, 'Mesa is more intuitive. A lot more flexible. Anyway, LonGen is a fantastic outfit to work for.'

'Oh, yeah, sure. Absolutely.'

'Welcome on board.'

'Lucky to get the job, I think anyway,' Sandip said.

'Just try to stay!'

Sandip frowned. 'Oh? Why do you say that?'

Walter sipped his water. 'Just they never do, the people in your job.'

'Really? How long did the last guy last?'

'About two months. The one before him, maybe less. Jeff, he was three ago — I liked him — he was nearly six months but he was the longest.'

'Where do they go?'

'Move on, I guess.'

This sounded ominous. 'Why do they go?'

'Not sure. They all said they liked it. Must have got a better offer, I guess. Maybe got headhunted.'

Sandip frowned. 'Do you keep in touch with them?'

Walter shook his head. 'No. Anyway, see you around.'

Sandip decided he would stay. The job was too good to quit. He was learning so much. It was a monumental step up from academia.

IN THE DAYS THAT FOLLOWED, SANDIP DECIDED HE QUITE LIKED HIS boss, Simon. At least he thought he did. Simon was hard to read. He always appeared calm, but gave the impression there was something going on he wasn't sharing. Sandip put it down to commercial secrets. Gene therapy was such a competitive industry, with so much potential. There were millions to be made, billions realistically. No wonder Simon kept himself to himself.   And also he was quite a sad guy. Walter told Sandip once that Simon was a widower. His wife had died in childbirth about ten years ago. He'd never remarried, just lived like a recluse in a huge white house in Holland Park.

Sandip had been there a month. He liked it. He was helping out on a couple of projects and on one of them working in a small team with the boss himself. They were working on a project, looking at correcting a genetic deficiency that caused a metabolic condition arising from a deficiency of acid alpha-glucosides. It was very exciting and the team was making substantial progress. Sandip liked to think he was making a contribution and the boss seemed pleased with him.

One day, it was the middle of November and Sandip had been working late. Everyone had gone home apart from Simon. Then at seven o'clock, Simon took off his gold-rimmed glasses and rubbed his eyes. 'That's all for tonight. Can't think straight anymore.'

Sandip laughed. He could have gone on longer. He was really engaged with the work. Simon said, 'Once again, really impressed by your drive to know. You really don't give up til you've delved into secrets, do you?'

'Gene therapy? No, I love it.'

Simon laughed. As they switched things off and got ready to go home, Simon said as if as an afterthought, 'Hey, Sandip. You go by Maida Vale to get home, don't you?'

'Yes, on my bike.'

'By the canal?'

'Usually, riding on the towpath is nicer than riding on the road.'

'Okay. You know I have a barge on the canal?'

Sandip shook his head. 'No, I didn't know that.'

'Nice to hang there sometimes. No phone, no internet. Just the water.'

'Yeah, sounds cool.' And Sandip thought one day he would have some kind of getaway place.

'I'm just not going there tonight. Just wondered if you could deliver something for me?'

'Sure. Of course. What is it?' Sandip thought he sounded too abrupt, so he said, 'But it's no problem'

'Great, the boat's called The Box of Delights. It's moored opposite John Masefield's House. Just a joke.'

'Ah.'

Simon peered at Sandip. Sandip didn't know why. Simon said, 'Masefield wrote The Box of Delights. One of my favourite books as a kid.'

'Okay. Sure.' Sandip had never heard of it.

'I just need you to take something. It's just a box. Just leave it on the barge, by the door into the cabin. There's a little roof thing that'll give it shelter.'

'Where will I get it?'

'It'll be downstairs.'

THE BOX WAS ABOUT A FOOT SQUARE, MADE OF THICK CARDBOARD. IT had 'The Box of Delights' written on it in Simon's handwriting. It lay ready for Sandip as he went out the front door, almost as if Simon had it put there before Sandip had even agreed. Not that Sandip minded being taken advantage of, if it led to promotion.

The grumpy security guard just grunted as Sandip took the box off the table. 'See you, George,' Sandip said as he put the box in his Fjellraven backpack.   George said nothing, not that he ever did, but Sandip had the weird feeling that George knew something about the box.

Outside, it was dark and damp. That miserable time in November before the Christmas lights go up. The bike ride up through Maida Vale was uneventful. The barge was moored by the canal that ran along Blomfield Road, and he found it easily enough. Even in the dark, he could see the boat was neatly painted and in good order. Sandip climbed off his bike and stepped on board and felt the boat sway slightly as he stepped on. He had the box in two hands. He wondered what was in it. As he moved it, whatever it contained seemed to roll like a cricket ball, but it wasn't as dense as that. Sandip shook his head. It didn't matter what it was. The cabin was below. He found the door and placed the box under the shelter of that half roof that covered the door so it wouldn't get wet if it rained. He was just stepping off the barge, when he was sure he heard something move below. It gave him a fright and he jumped then he laughed at himself but he still got off the barge in a hurry, picked up his bike and stood listening.

Standing on the towpath, mounted on his bike, he could have sworn the movement came from the hold of the barge, but there were no lights on. That was horrible enough, but then he told himself it was just rats or something. Horrible enough, but completely natural.

NOTHING MUCH HAPPENED FOR THE NEXT COUPLE OF WEEKS. IT WAS the beginning of December. The office had its Christmas decorations up and people were looking forward to the office Christmas party at a very nice restaurant, all food and drink paid for by Simon. One night just before that, Sandip was working late. Simon was still around. He made a point of coming to Sandip's desk. 'Hey,' he said. 'Thanks for delivering that package. Sorry I forgot to thank you before.'

'No worries, boss. Not a problem.'

'Weren't you curious what was in the box?'

Sandip shrugged.

Simon's grin grew. 'Come on, you with your lust for knowledge. You must have been tempted to take a peek inside.'

Sandip shook his head determinedly. 'No, not really. None of my business.'

Simon was teasing him. 'But how would I have known? You could have got away with it.'

Sandip wondered if this was all some kind of test of integrity. He laughed. 'No, honestly. Your business is your business.'

Simon laughed and clapped him on the shoulder. 'Only messing with you. But...' He paused and grinned. 'Just wondered if you'd do it again?'

Sandip frowned involuntarily, then corrected that and said, 'What?'

'Take another package.'

'Sure, of course. It's on my way home.'

'That's what I thought. Same deal as before.'

SO SANDIP PICKED UP THE NEW PACKAGE UNDER THE WATCHFUL EYE of George the guard, put it in his Fjellraven backpack and pedalled through London streets festooned with Christmas lights, all the house windows glittering with lighted trees.

He found the barge again and remembered the feeling that there was something in there, something moving about in the dark. It was with some trepidation that he took the box and stepped onto the deck. He put down the box. Whatever it contained, half-rolled again. He put the box down, listening for movement below deck, but heard nothing.

When he stepped back on the towpath, he noticed his fingers were wet. Some sticky liquid. It looked dark, but in the coloured lights along the towpath he couldn't make out the colour. It was maybe oil or perhaps instant coffee. Whatever it was, it had come out of the box. He hoped he hadn't broken whatever was in there and felt a flash of anxiety at the thought. But he'd been careful. Still, he didn't want to upset Simon. He wiped his hands on a bunch of wet leaves.

· · ·

SIMON DIDN'T MENTION THE ERRAND AGAIN OR SAY THANK YOU until January. Sandip had been at LonGen for nearly three months now. They'd worked late after Christmas, but no requests to deliver any boxes. Not until the third week of January. It was the same as before. Sandip agreed. After all, it was no skin off his nose.

'Still didn't peek in the box?' Simon said.

'No, Mr Wroxhall.'

'Call me Simon, please. We've known each other long enough now. Anyway, the box will be downstairs.'

THIS TIME SANDIP STARED AT THE BOX BEFORE PICKING IT UP. THERE was nothing leaking through it. Nothing to stain his fingers. Middle-aged George sat there behind his glass, still saying nothing. Sandip picked up the box and put it in his rucksack. As he always did, he said good night to George. This time George said, 'See you, kid.' It amazed Sandip that George actually spoke. He even sounded kind. Sandip's jaw nearly dropped. The look on George's face was difficult to read — sad? Almost pitying? What the hell did that mean?

And then he was out in the night on his bike, the box bumping against his empty sandwich box and water bottle in the rucksack as he rode. No Christmas lights now, the year had turned January dark, everything hunkered down awaiting the coming of spring. But spring was a long way off yet.

Sandip got off the road and went on cycle paths where he could. Round here they sometimes coincided with the towpath. The wind was cold. The water was dark and the barges moored alongside the canal all sat in darkness. He pedalled on. He just wanted to get home now. Something about George speaking to him unnerved him. It wasn't usual. And then that thing rolling around in the box. What the actual hell was it? The first couple of times he hadn't been bothered, but now the weirdness of this repeated errand was like an itch he couldn't scratch. It just piqued his curiosity. He remembered what Simon had said after the first time. He could look in and Simon probably wouldn't know. Then he thought it was a clever double bluff. It must be a test. He sighed. He really wanted to know what was in the box though.

He got to Blomfield Road and the Box of Delights. The barge sat there in the dark, quiet and still, floating on the dark canal, moored with ropes to the bank. Sandip got off his bike and unslung the rucksack from his back. That damn thing was rolling around in the box. What was it? He took out the box and put his rucksack down on the floor.

Then he heard it. The same noise he'd heard the first time. There was definitely something moving about in the barge. From the noise it made, and the way the boat rolled in the water, it was heavier than a rat. Sandip listened hard. He heard it scuttling around. His heart went crazy. Bigger than a rat. It might be a dog. Maybe Simon kept his dog there? But that made no sense. It was cruel. Simon wasn't cruel.

Whatever it was down there moved again, and this time he heard it moan. It was an indistinct noise. Animal-like, but not quite. It was no dog or cat. But there was definitely something living in that barge.

Sandip swallowed hard. He just had to put the box on the barge and leave. He bent down and got the box. He didn't step onto the barge itself, just leaned down and placed the box on the barge, just on the deck. Then he stood back, breathing heavily. That would do.

The thing in the box rolled inside. Two mysteries. Something in the box and something in the barge. They were obviously related somehow. He couldn't get into the barge to find out, but he could take a peek in the box. He shouldn't do it. Of course he shouldn't but wondering what it was that he'd brought three times was driving him mad.

Then the thing in the hold moved again. Something about it being down there in the dark scared him. He went to pick up his bike, then rain fell pitter-patter into the water, onto the barge and onto his face. He looked up at the invisible clouds. The rain pattered on the cardboard box. It would soak it through where it was. Sandip sighed. Simon had told him to put it under the little roof thing to keep it out of the rain.

He put the bike down, stepped forward and picked up the box. He was going to have to step onto the barge. He hadn't heard the noise for a while. That's what frightened him. But now there was just the lapping of the water and the soft drizzle of rain. No moving, no moaning. He began to think he'd imagined the weird noises from inside the barge. In any case, he had to put the box in shelter so it didn't get soaked.

Sandip stepped onto the barge and felt it move under his feet. Steadying himself, he got to the middle of the deck. The boat rocked. The thing in the box rolled with it. Whatever was in there was actually quite heavy and dense seeming. What the hell was it? The lid wasn't sealed down, probably deliberately. Like Sandip had thought all along, it was probably a test. But then again, Simon wouldn't know he'd looked. Even if it was an integrity thing, he could just lie. It wasn't like he liked lying. He'd rather not lie, but his curiosity was driving him crazy. Here he was standing on a narrow boat in the dark in January going insane wanting to know what was in the box. It was easy done. He'd look, then go. It was just all this unknowing that was unnerving him. He owed it to his sanity and his anxiety to just look in the box, see it was nothing, then close the lid and leave.

Still, he hesitated, the box still in his hands. The rain fell. A car went by on the road on the other side of the canal. A noise, maybe an imagined noise, from the towpath. He snapped his head round. He was getting very jittery. Just shadows. Then he peered. Was there someone there? But now it was silent. Just him and the box. Just a peek, then he'd go.

Damn it. He tried to leave. He sighed and bent down, the rain cold on his face. The box was getting soaked by him just standing there holding it. If he wasn't going to look, he just needed to put it by the barge door under the little roof.

He shook his head then placed the box by the barge door, just in shelter.

And then he bent to open the box.

He had failed the test, but so what? Then he noticed the barge door was ajar. That was weird. That hadn't happened before. He stood up and stepped back. The door moved a little. Maybe the wind. But there was no wind. He sensed it watching him. There was something in there. The door opened a little more on its own. He was frozen to the spot. There was definitely something in there, something coming up the steps. Something that had been in the hold. Whatever it was, it breathed.

Sandip freaked out. Jumped, turned and tripped over his own feet in his panic to get away. He kicked as he tumbled send the box skidding. The top flew off and the contents rolled out. A misshapen sticky ball rolled over the deck and nudged him in the ribs. It was soft and squishy and wet. It was about the size of a cricket ball. Even in the gloom, he saw it had tubes protruding that were cut off. Sandip screamed and scrabbled to get up and away from it. He flailed in his panic. It was a heart, a bloody, cold heart.

Then, the thing from below came out of the cabin door. He couldn't make out clearly what it was. Something with long bony hands and damp palms that grabbed him and pulled him, trying to tug him by his foot, trying to drag him below.

Sandip shrieked again, but screams on London nights often go ignored. No one wants to get involved.

The thing pulled him and dragged him and drew him in. He felt its strong hands on his ankles and calves and knees as it reeled him towards it and then heaved him down into the dark cabin, banging his head and shoulders on the wooden steps as he went. Then when it had him at the bottom, it stopped. He heard its ragged breathing. He felt its clammy breath and then a light flicked on.

Simon Wroxhall sat there in the cabin of the barge. Near him, holding Sandip tight, vile and leathery and misshapen, was a thing that might once have been human. Maybe. Now it was an abomination, with a slavering mouth filled with yellow diseased teeth and watery idiot eyes.

Simon gave a slow handclap. 'Well done, Sandip. You did better than all the others. You never actually opened the box. I thought your curiosity would make you, but it didn't.'

The monstrous thing snuffled and giggled.

'But it doesn't matter. The main thing is you're here.'

'I don't understand,' Sandip said.

'It's quite simple,' Simon said. 'This is one of my earlier experiments. It didn't go as I planned, but I love him, anyway. He usually only gets hearts to eat. Fresh meat is a treat. He got a taste for it when he ate his mother.'

The rheumy eyed thing, looked at its father as if for permission.

Simon nodded. 'Yes, baby. Tea time.'

❧ 10 ❧

GEMATRIA

'Honestly, love, it doesn't actually mean you're going to die.'

The card reader had just turned over the Death card: Number 13 in the Tarot Pack. There on the card was a skull, with roses coming out of the empty eye sockets, painted lusciously in crimson, black and gold. The reader was smiling, and then, as she pulled the next card and revealed it with a flourish of her elegant black-gelled finger nails, the psychic gave a brief sigh. 'Number 16 now — The Tower Struck Down.'

Alicia Symonds, pretty and petite, well-turned out and generally wise to the world, knew enough about the tarot to see she had just been dealt death and destruction one after the other. The psychic sat back and smiled, abandoning the cards on her red-velvet tablecloth. The room they sat in was in the basement of a psychic shop near Victoria, London. More Pimlico, to be honest. An incense stick burned, sending a straight column of Palo Santo scented smoke to the dirty ceiling. The place here was pretty cool, the psychic, Roseanne, was pretty cool: Alicia had good reports of her from her friend Emily. Roseanne's lips were painted crimson, her eyes kohled to within an inch of their life, and full black hair that fell in dreadlocks down her back.

Roseanne said, 'No, love. People get this wrong. The Death card doesn't mean a literal death; it means an ending. And the Tower is a sudden change of state. Nothing to worry about.'

But Alicia was still uneasy.

'And remember,' Roseanne said, 'What's meant for you won't go past you.' She leant forward and put her hand on Alicia's. 'I'm talking about the love interest.'

That's why Alicia had visited her in the first place. There was a guy at work: terribly artistic, dark-haired, black hair on his forearms as he played his guitar. He was in a band and Alicia and the work girls had gone to see them play in Camden. She thought he liked her, but wasn't sure; hence the visit to Pimlico.

Alicia sighed. 'I hope you're right,' Fortunately, these thoughts of Michel (he was French) had driven previous worries about the Death Card from her mind. Number 13: unlucky for some.

Alicia paid via Roseanne's portable card reader, picked up her bag and just as she was leaving the room, Roseanne said haltingly, 'Another thing. I sense flowers.' Then she smiled. 'Yes, you'll definitely be sent some flowers today.'

That put a spring in Alicia's step. She hoped the flowers were from Michel. It was Friday and she had a day off. She worked as a nurse at the Royal Free at Hampstead and Michel was one of the gastro registrars there, as well as being the lead guitarist of an Indie band.

As she came out of Roseanne's flat, the weather was foul. Rain drove across the sky, sending Alicia scurrying into the shelter of nearby buildings. She glanced back. The house she'd just come out of was at number thirteen. She laughed to herself as she put up her umbrella. Stupid. It was just that she was sensitised to the number thirteen and she was seeing it everywhere.

It was certainly no day for wandering around Central London so she thought she'd go back home to North Finchley. She had plenty of time and she quite liked going overground so she planned to catch the bus rather than the tube home. She'd decided she would start to keep a journal, so she popped into a Paperchase and got a Leuchturm dotted one. She went to the counter and paid with a card.

'Sixteen pounds,' the assistant said.

Alicia paid with her card. Sixteen quid was a bit steep. But it was Paperchase and it was Leuchturm and it was Victoria Station so what did she expect?

She got herself a coffee, which again was expensive, and sipped it while she waited for the bus. The bus came, a big red double decker. It would take her all the way home to North Finchley from Victoria and then as she read the destination on the front she realised it was a Number 13. She felt a twinge of anxiety. It didn't mean anything. It was just a coincidence. She'd caught this bus before and nothing had happened. She paid with her Oyster Card. She didn't know how much she had left on it, and she didn't want to check in case it was £13.

After loading up, the bus started off. It was an electric bus and very quiet as it went down behind Buckingham Palace. Alicia put her earphones in and watched the rain streak down the bus windows. There was something melancholy and nice about drifting through London, stopping and starting, knowing she had ages before she had to get off. They stopped at Grosvenor Square, by the American Embassy. British police with machine guns stood on the corners. Closer to the embassy, armed US marines were positioned around the building and above them US flags fluttered in the wind.

Idly, she looked at the flag. It was very colourful with the stars and stripes.

Idly, she counted the stripes. She knew it before she finished: there were thirteen of them. Her heart beat faster. Why couldn't she get the number thirteen out of her head?

She googled the American flag. Apparently the thirteen stripes were for the original thirteen colonies when they broke free of Britain. See, perfectly rational! She told herself. But she still couldn't swallow properly. She felt hot. All these thirteens were just a coincidence. Like she'd already decided, it was just because she was sensitised to it.

Alicia thought about getting off the number 13 bus. Maybe seeing these thirteens was a sign that it would have a crash? But that was stupid. It was just superstition. There was nothing intrinsic about the number thirteen that made it unlucky. Just an old wives' tale. Still, she felt her palms go clammy.

. . .

AT HYDE PARK CORNER A STUDENT CAME AND SAT NEXT TO HER, wearing a black donkey-jacket type coat that was wet with rain. He was apologetic and though he'd taken in her looks, was well-mannered and ignored her rather than staring or trying to make conversation. She could tell he was a student because he was reading a big textbook as he sat on the bus. Her mind calmed as it mused about the student. Then she saw the book was about mathematics. Something about the Fibonacci Sequence. She'd heard of it but knew nothing about it.

The student flicked through the pages; he wasn't reading it properly, just skimming. It looked like he had just got the book because he was at the start. She looked and saw that he had his finger on the page to hold it down and she could see from where she sat that it was page thirteen.

Thirteen. A sign. This was totally nuts. Alicia cleared her throat. She had to know. 'Excuse me,' she said.

The student looked at her and blinked with soft cow brown eyes. He wasn't handsome, but he seemed nice. From his expression he couldn't believe that a pretty blonde girl had started a conversation with him. 'Yes?' he said.

'What's the Fibonacci Sequence?'

'Ah,' the student said with a grin. Not only was this bonny blonde girl talking to him, but she was interested in maths! He began a long, overly detailed explanation. Alicia felt panic in her fingers and in her chest. 'Just tell me?'

'What?' he said.

'Is thirteen a Fibonacci number?'

He nodded. 'Yes, the numbers are 0, 1, 1, 2, 3, 5, 8, 13. You get them by adding the previous two together. Except for zero, of course. So the next would be...'

Then she remembered today was Friday the Thirteenth.

Alicia abruptly stood. 'Excuse me.' She had to get off. She couldn't think straight. Her pulse pounded in her ears.

'Of course,' the student said bewildered and moved as she pushed past him. Alicia pressed the button that indicated to the driver that she wanted to get off.

They were on Park Road, just running west of Regent's Park. She scanned her memory of London geography. She could walk down Regent's Canal and get to Camden and take the Northern Line up to North Finchley.

She stepped off the Number 13 bus with a palpable sense of relief. It was drizzling, but she had her coat and her umbrella. She knew that you could get to the canal towpath across the road to the right. The entrance was between two buildings and hard to see. She peered through the rain and nearly went past it, but she saw a wooden finger-post with the number sixteen cycle route marked on it for Camden. At least it wasn't number thirteen cycle route. She wouldn't have walked there if it was.

Soon Alicia was walking alongside the Regent's Canal. The canal was full of drifting autumn leaves. There was the odd jogger and a barge sailed past her at one point, chugging along with its diesel engine.

Alicia had her head down. The weather was so bad she knew it would be dark soon. But she just had to walk along the canal and then get up by the Zoo bridge so she could walk on to Camden Town tube. At least the tube trains didn't have numbers.

As she walked, she thought about how she'd spooked herself. These past few days she'd been uncharacteristically nervous. She should maybe see someone about it. She knew Andrea from psych liaison at work. But all these thirteens were just stupid. She would just pull herself together and it would be fine.

There seemed fewer people now. The weather seemed to have put the runners off and there were no more barges going by. The canal path lay with a steep grassy bank to the left behind a scrubby screen of trees. On the right were some grand houses and then she came within sight of the zoo. The animals were keeping out of the rain too.

It smelled old and damp, of leaves and soil and wood and dank canals. She shivered. It was getting colder. The clouds lay heavy above and there was no sign of the rain easing off. In fact, it seemed to be getting heavier. She hurried on.

Alicia shuddered as she saw two brown rats scuttle off to the left.

This canal path went on for ages. She didn't remember it being so long. A sense of doom fell over her. She felt as if something dreadful was going to happen. She told herself it was all psychological and that a chat with Andrea would put it into perspective.

Still the Tarot Death card — number 13, on Friday 13th and then the Number 13 bus. It was freaky.

The grey concrete animal houses of the zoo on the right-hand bank had spaces for the animals to come out right down to the canal. Most of the animals were in. There were some ring-tailed lemurs out. She would not google how many rings the lemurs had on their tails. She almost did, but she told herself it was stupid. What if it was thirteen, so what? This was just her nerves playing tricks on her. She got to the floating Chinese restaurant and this was where she left the canal towpath and came up to street level.

She was soaked despite her coat and umbrella. The rain just wouldn't give up. She walked along St Mark's Square. She would have to dry off a little and catch the tube a bit later. She nipped into a cafe bar to her left, shaking her umbrella into an umbrella stand and hanging up her coat on the peg.

'Terrible weather,' the barman said. He was handsome. Looked Greek. Dark like Michel, but heavier built. She smiled to herself. Then she remembered what Roseanne the psychic had said about her getting flowers. That cheered her up.

'Had an enjoyable day?' the barman said.

'Awful.'

He laughed. 'I won't ask. What can I get you?'

Alicia thought. She recognised the song in the background as being by Neil Sedaka. The barman mouthed the words absent mindedly as he waited for her order. 'Happy birthday Sweet Sixteen...'

She said, 'You know what? It's my day off. I'm wet and pissed off so I'll have a beer.' It was unusual for her to have a beer, but somehow this particular beer was calling to her.

'A beer? What would you like?"

She knew what she wanted. The beer with the nice blue and gold label. She didn't know what it was, but somehow that's the one she wanted.

'That one,' she said.

'Ah, Kronenburg 1664. That's nice,' the barman said.

'Yes. I'll have that.'

'So, some sixteen sixty-four?' He emphasised the number, as if she didn't look like a Kronenburg drinker.

Alicia frowned. 'I'm not usually a beer drinker, but I just fancy it.'

'Must be calling out to you.'

He poured the cold beer and she drank half of it straight off. Then she swallowed the rest.

'You were thirsty. Want another?'

'No, actually, I better be going.'

'My loss.'

She laughed and went to pay with a card, but it wasn't authorised. 'Sorry,' she said.

He said, 'Probably our machine.'

She said, 'Trouble is, I don't have any cash.'

'There's a cash machine over the road.'

'Okay. I'll just nip out.'

'Sure.'

Then at the door she said, 'I will come back. I won't run off without paying'

'Sure, sure.'

She blushed. 'Honestly.'

'Don't worry, I've got your number.'

She thought he was serious, then saw his grin. 'Be right back,' she said, grabbing her umbrella because it was still raining.

THE MACHINE WAS ON THE OTHER SIDE OF THE ROAD. ALICIA PICKED her way through the stream of cars to cross the street, got to the machine and put in her pin. And as she did so, the coincidence of numbers struck her again. Her card pin was 1316. She shuddered, snatched the cash and tried to laugh it off. Turning back, Alicia got to the kerb and looked both ways. An unexpected gust of wind turned her umbrella inside out, making unable to see at the instant she stepped out onto the road.

The van hit her. It was going too fast. She wasn't looking. It was a flower delivery van. It braked, lost control, skidded and slammed into her, the door coming open, spilling flowers all over. The van's registration number was TWR 16S.

Stricken and dying, covered in bloody flowers, Alicia had visions of Death and the Tower Struck Down, card number 13 and card number 16. And she heard Roseanne the psychic's words echoing in her ears. 'Yes, you'll definitely be sent some flowers today.'

11

HE WAITS

My name is Theresa Schulz. I'm a psychotherapist. One of the strangest cases I ever dealt with was that of Melissa Hall. A friend recommended me to her and she came for therapy that Fall. I rent a consulting-room just by Harley Street in London, so my clients tend to be well off. Melissa was a banker. She was stylish and wore expensive but tasteful clothes — understated in the way the polite rich have. I usually open up with a simple "So?" But sometimes people take a while to talk. She was one of those.

She hesitated a long time, as if gathering her thoughts, or her courage, then she said," I know you'll think me silly," and stopped, almost as if frightened to go on. I felt like saying that I'd heard some very strange things and I doubted that anything could shock me. Or at least I believed that before I met Melissa.

Eventually she said, "It's a dream. I've had it for years and it keeps coming back."

I sat there in the relaxed and interested silence that we therapists practice so hard to maintain. But she still waited.

"Go on," I said, finally. "I'm interested." And I offered her some water. She drank it then said, "It's a nice place here. A nice address — near Harley Street."

I smiled and said, "I think you're avoiding telling me about your dream."

But she kept avoiding. She said, "I'm from London. But you're not. You're American by your accent..."

"From New York. But I've been here several years now."

She laughed - a nervous sound - but continued. "Yes, the dream. It's taken me such a lot of courage to come here; I don't want to mess it up by being too scared to tell you." She looked at me as if seeking reassurance. I smiled and shrugged. It was up to her whether she told me or not.

"It goes back to when I was at school. I came from a poor area in East London — South of the River. I couldn't always afford clothes like this. My father was a van driver. My mother worked in a button factory. At least we had lots of buttons!" she laughed. I waited.

"So anyway, my primary school. The dream didn't come until after I'd left. I was about 15 when I first had it."

"Describe it."

"Well, I'm back at my school. There is an eerie atmosphere, as if we know something awful is going to happen. The children are in the classroom standing around, not knowing what to do. The teachers..." she shuddered and put her hand to her face. But she got her courage. "I don't like talking about this."

"You're doing fine. But you can stop whenever you want."

"No, I don't want to stop. The teachers are all locked in the staff room; they've locked themselves in. They're looking out through the window into the classroom. But they're locked in as if they are not going to help. There are ten of us in the classroom."

"You seem very precise about that."

"No, definitely ten. I know them all. Anyway, the teachers are just staring at us in some kind of dreadful helpless horror. They know what's going to happen but they can't do anything about it. And the kids are there too. We know something is coming, but we're bewildered. We're only kids. How can we stop it?"

She was shaking. I put my hand out to touch hers. To comfort her. "If it's too painful - stop. We can talk about it next time."

"No, I can't stop. I've stirred it up by talking about it. I can't lock it back up."

I sat in what I hoped was an encouraging and supportive quiet. I wanted her to know I was there for her, professionally, as her therapist.

Falteringly she started again. "And then the door to the classroom opens behind us. I don't see what it is at first. But I'm looking at Tom - Tom Morton. He has such terror on his face. I've never seen anything like it. He's staring at the door. Looking at what comes in. And everything's slow. The children try to run. I see the teachers, turning away. Almost embarrassed that they're going to let this thing happen. And Tommy is screaming, but it's slowed down - like a tape. I sense something behind me. Something comes in through the door. The other children can see it and they're screaming, terrified. They try to run, but they're so slow, and there are no doors out anyway. Only the one that has opened and the one into the teachers' room that they've locked shut. I sense this thing behind me. And then I see its hands reaching to take Tommy. And then I wake up. And I'm always terrified. I'm shaking and I put all the lights on and I'm too scared to sleep again."

"So you didn't see this thing?"

She shook her head. She was crying - slight, frightened sobs. I handed her a tissue and she wiped her eyes.

"What about the hands? What were they like?"

She shook her head again. "I don't know. I can't remember. Maybe there weren't hands. It's as if it's too frightening to remember." She laughed. "Stupid aren't I?"

"Not at all. So what happened to Tom Morton? In real life?"

"I never saw him again. Remember I'd already left my primary school by the time I had the dream first. He went to an all boys secondary school."

"So he's ok?"

"No. That's what made me so scared of the dream. He was killed."

"When?"

"Shortly after I had the dream first - when he was taken in the dream. His death was in the papers. He was run over on a pedestrian crossing."

"That's sad," I said.

She nodded. "It is. But it's just a coincidence of course."

"You say that with some hesitation."

"It must be a coincidence. What do you think?"

"I think it must be a coincidence."

She smiled. "Thank God."

"But you had the dream again?"

"I did. I would have it once a year. Maybe only once every two years or even longer. If there was a long gap, I thought I'd got rid of it and started to be happy. As if a cloud lifted from me — a darkness. But then the dream returned and I was turned into the same shivering wreck I'd always been."

"So was it always the same?"

"Mostly. But not quite. Each time it happened the children were older. They aged with me, so I saw them as adults eventually. But the teachers didn't age. They were just the same."

"And you never saw the thing that came in?"

"No, I always woke up. But..."

"But?"

"Every time it came it took one of us."

"And you thought the person really died?"

She nodded. "Stupid. But it scares me."

"And did they die?"

She shrugged. "It's now been nearly twenty years since I first had the dream. I've lost contact with them all. I know that my friend Sarah. She was my best friend back then. She died of leukaemia. But that's just a coincidence again, isn't it?"

I nodded. "Of course. How could it be anything else? What about the others?"

"Well, as I said, I lost contact with them."

"Why don't you find out?"

"How?"

"Well, mutual friends. Facebook. Friends Reunited? There are websites for this kind of thing. I don't think anyone can disappear these days."

"Do you think I should?"

I said, "I use different kinds of therapies, but one of them - a very popular one - is Cognitive Behavioural Therapy. In this, if we have irrational thoughts, we challenge them. We look for evidence. Sometimes we can set up little experiments to see whether our irrational fears have any basis."

"So you think I should try and contact them?"

"I'm not pushing you at all. But it would be one way to show that this dream is just a nasty scary dream. It's not real. It has no power in the real world."

She looked hopeful. Her face brightened. "That would be so good. I've let this thing dominate my life for too long."

She talked of some other things, her mother, her friends. She had never married but had a good social life, spending the money she earned on skiing trips and scuba diving in the Maldives. I arranged I would see her the next week.

That night, I was home on time for a change. My husband Michael made dinner and we sat down with a nice bottle of French wine.

"Good day?" he asked.

"Yeah, ok," I smiled. "I had a weird case. You know usually it's anxiety and depression, but this time it's a woman who has a recurring dream."

"One that bothers her?" he said without looking up.

"Sure. Lots." I told him the gist of the dream.

"Creepy," he said. "What's the matter with her?"

"Well, I think she has a psychosis. Just it's contained in the dream so it doesn't erupt into her life. The dream's very therapeutic really. Stops her going crazy for real."

"Like an abscess. The body keeps all the poison wrapped up in a neat bubble." Michael's a doctor - he thinks bodies, I think minds.

"Like that," I agreed.

"So what are you going to do?"

"Well I'm not going to dig too much. Just stay on the surface and maybe try out some behavioural experiments so she can challenge her fears with evidence."

"Sounds good. More wine?"

"Always more wine, Michael. You know me."

The next week Melissa came back. If anything she was worse than the first week, but she didn't hesitate before talking. She accepted the water and then when we sat down, she said, "So, I looked people up. I did what you said. I joined the classmates reunited sites and checked friends of friends on Facebook."

"And?"

"I didn't find out about everyone."

"Of course. Some may have left the country."

"Sure."

Her complexion was grey.

"So, did it help?" I prompted. "Did it show you that when they disappear in the dream, they don't disappear in life?"

She shook her head. "Not really. I didn't manage to find anyone of the ten who was in that class with me."

I waited for her to go on.

"But I found people who knew about some of them."

"And what did they say?"

She looked terrified. "They've gone. The ones I managed to trace are all dead."

"That can't be."

"It is. And I'm sure that they died just after I dreamt they were taken in that room."

"But that isn't rational." I began to wonder if talking to me about the dream had in some way unlocked the psychosis. They couldn't all be dead, but it was certain she believed they were and that their deaths were connected to her dream. I considered referring her to a psychiatrist I knew who could prescribe her some anti-psychotic medication.

She blurted, "You've got to help me."

Unusually for me — I tend to keep the distance — but I was moved by the emotional state she was in, I took her hand and stroked it, like a mother might. "I will. Listen this will all be ok. It's just a nightmare. It can't have any affect on the real world. If some of your friends are dead, then it's a sad coincidence. Others of them will be in Australia or California, enjoying the sunshine. Don't worry."

"But it's worse than I told you," she said.

"Why?" I tried to sound comforting, but I was seriously worried about her mental state.

"It's worse because, they're all gone. I'm the only one left in the room. The next time I dream it, he'll take me." She broke down into horror stricken sobbing. She was almost coughing with the depths of her sobs. I tried to comfort her as best I could. I'm not a big believer in medication but I thought a dose of valium right now would help her. I told her I would get something and I went over to the landline and rang my psychiatrist friend Martin. He has a surgery just on Harley Street. He was a very expensive doctor, but we got on well. He was free and he agreed to come over. He wrote her up for something that would help her nerves and help her sleep. She hadn't been sleeping until exhaustion dragged her there every night. She was scared of dreaming.

As I said, I think medication has its place, but the real cure for these fears is to face them. We arranged to meet in two days. She was grateful and thanked me as she left my consulting room.

I was going to set up an experiment. She had told me the name of the school and by looking on the Internet, I saw that it still existed. I thought if we could go there, in the cold light of day and she could see it was only a school. Just an ordinary school, that would help take away the supernatural dread that haunted her. I learned in fact that the school was shut. It was due to be sold off for re-development into executive homes. But it was still owned by the local Borough Council. After spending what seemed hours on the phone and talking to a string of people, I finally got hold of the school's headmistress. The story was that the Council was selling off the old building and was using the money to fund a new one. The kids had already moved, but the head-mistress had the keys to the old place. I explained who I was and I explained Melissa's story. She was interested. I mentioned no names because of client confidentiality. Of course she didn't know her; she'd only been there seven years. She was very reluctant.

I said, "If we could just have the keys, so that she can go to the old classroom and see that it's just a room. That there is nothing fearful about it."

She hesitated. "I'm not sure. There's no insurance."

I said, "We're both professional women. We're not going to have a party. It'll be fine. And of course if there is anything your new school needs, by way of a small donation. Books perhaps? Sports equipment?"

"Well, the football team does need a new strip..."

"Fine. I'll pay for that."

The truth was I was going to be a little out of pocket. But I wanted to help Melissa. She was in such a state and I must admit I'd become curious myself. I believed in my therapies and I knew it could cure her.

When I was home, Michael had cooked again. He supported me as he always did. "So what's the plan?"

"Well, I want to get the keys and just spend some time there."

"Sure."

"I thought overnight."

"Overnight?" He was incredulous. "Why do you need to go there overnight?"

"I want her to sleep there. And dream there. And even if she has the dream, especially if she has the dream, it'll prove to her there's no basis for her fears. They call it immersion. It's a technique. And it works."

He shrugged. "You know best. But if it was me..."

"It's not you. I am going to cure this girl."

"Ok but keep your cell phone on. Do you have a date for going there?"

I nodded.

When I told Melissa, she started shaking.

I said, "Listen, hon, it's the only way. We've got to get you through this. Trust me. It's a tried and tested technique. You need to be free of this."

"But to stay there?"

"To sleep there. To dream. To prove it's nonsense."

"Oh God, I'm so scared."

I put my hand on hers. "Trust me Melissa. I'm going to make you better."

When the time finally came, I drove Melissa to the school. It was still light. The area was poor and broken down. She said, "I haven't been here since my mother died. No reason to. I'd forgotten how dirty it was."

"It's just a poor working class area. Nothing wrong with that," I said. "That it?"

I pointed to a red brick, Victorian building. It was obviously a school but there was a 'For Sale' sign up on it that had a 'S old' poster pasted across. She stiffened and nodded.

"Ok, I've got the keys." I parked pretty much outside. The area was quiet. Newspapers blew down the gutters. A stray cat walked across the road. Two youths stood on the street corner, hoods up, smoking, watching my BMW.

"Just a sec." I got out, engine still running, and stepped up to the metal gates. There was a heavy chain round them, which I unlocked. I pushed the gates open then went back to the car. I drove it through into the yard and locked the gates behind us. At least that would keep them from stealing my car.

Melissa got out and just stared up at the dirty windows of the old building. "I had some nice times here when I was a kid," she said.

"See?" I said. "Here help me with these."

I had come well prepared. I had two sleeping bags, two air mattresses, an iPod docking station and an electric fire. I had insisted that the headmistress switch on the electricity supply even if she wouldn't agree to heat the whole school. She agreed and said that was fair enough.

Melissa helped me in with the stuff. Lugging it seemed to distract her and help her mood.

"Where's the classroom?" I said.

She pointed up the stairs. "Up there. First floor."

"First floor?" Then I remembered Europeans call the real first floor the "Ground Floor" so their first floor is really the second. I knew that. "Ok," I said. "Up we go."

The classroom was locked but the headmistress had given me a big bunch of keys. I searched through them until I found the right one. Inside, I switched on the electric light.

"Jesus, it looks just the same," she said.

There were a few desks still in the room and the kids chairs pushed up against the wall in a big pile. There was indeed a kind of teachers' observation room with a door leading off and a window so they could see what the kids were doing. I went in. There was a sink and a dead mouse on the floor. The water was still on. I pushed the mouse to the side with my foot.

"I'm not going to sleep here. I can't," said Melissa.

"What did I say about trusting me? Anyway, I've come prepared. Look!" I pulled out the hip flask that Michael had bought me for when we went country walking in the English shires. "Brandy!" I said.

And soon we made the place cosy. I put the heater on; we laid the mattresses on the floor - after finding a brush and sweeping it - and we put the sleeping bags on top of them. I put on the iPod and soon we were listening to silly happy pop music and talking about places we'd been and I told her about the old boyfriend I'd really loved who was a painter. That was before I met Michael. And then I noticed her eyes beginning to get heavy. The brandy and my reassuring company were doing the trick. I turned the music off. She was breathing lightly, eyes closed. And then it was just a question of sleeping till the morning. I left the light on in the classroom to reassure her if she woke up. I was making a big enough donation; they could afford to leave one lousy electric light bulb burning all night. I went and brushed my teeth in the sink. I would have to do without a shower but it was for a good cause. As quietly as I could, I got into my sleeping bag beside Melissa. She was flat out. And then I dozed and slept.

When I awoke it had that feeling of the middle of the night. The light was still on. Melissa was deep asleep. I lay there. And I heard the annoying drip-drip-drip of the tap in the teacher's adjoining room. I hadn't turned it off properly. I got up in my pyjamas and went to fix it. As I got into the room with its dripping tap and dead mouse, the door clicked shut behind me. It was on a latch on the other side. There was a keyhole this side, but I'd left the bunch of keys with my stuff beside the sleeping Melissa.

I looked through the glass. I was debating on whether I should thump it and wake her up or just wait it out till morning.

And then the atmosphere grew strange. I got scared. I turned to look at the classroom door. It was opening, slowly, but deliberately.

From where I was, I couldn't see what was opening the door, but a rush of helpless fear kept me staring — knowing I couldn't help.

I watched as the door opened, still hiding what was behind it - hiding who was pushing it. I saw Melissa wake suddenly. I saw her mouth open to scream. But the noise was muted behind the glass panel. I saw her turn and see the door opening. She looked at me — wordlessly begging for my help. I saw her nightmare come into the room and crawl towards her, reaching with its black twisted hands. She tried to fight it - tried to push it off, but she couldn't. It enveloped her. I saw its pointed fingernails and long ragged hair, flapping in the unfelt wind.

I must have fainted, or passed out in terror. When I woke it was day. I was still in the adjoining room. I found an old fashioned iron — a solid block of metal dating from around 1910, and I smashed the lock off. Melissa wasn't there. Nothing of her was there. I ran round the school looking and yelling in every room — in every corridor. But she was gone. It had taken her.

I never saw Melissa Hall again. I was investigated by the Police, but it was obvious I'd committed no crime. Thanks to Michael's job, and my insurance I could afford to take a year off. After that, I felt better. I even started working again.

I don't like to sleep any more — not now. Because I've dreamed of it. In my dream I'm sitting in my consulting room. Just like I had been with Melissa, but she's gone. Then I see the door opening.

12

THE GOLDEN SAXOPHONE

'They stole my saxophone!' Isaac yelled out. He couldn't believe it. He looked and looked for it but it was gone.

They had their gear in the back of a van and had gone for a bacon sandwich, leaving the van unlocked. The thieves had been in a hurry so they grabbed the closest things and one of those was Isaac's sax.

They were *The Golden Void,* a psychedelic band that were going to make it big soon. It was 1972; Wishbone Ash had just released *Argus,* Genesis *Foxtrot* and Jethro Tull *Thick as a Brick.* Issac saw himself as a rival to Ian Anderson except he didn't stand on one leg when he played, wasn't famous and played the saxophone rather than the flute. Maybe he was more like Hawkwind's Nik Turner, who did play saxophone? But he wasn't going to be anything now because his sax had been stolen and he had no money to buy a replacement.

Isaac was eighteen and he'd just left school and was picking up bits of work here and there, which suited him because it gave him more time to focus on his music, but it didn't leave him with a lot of spare cash.

The Void were doing free gigs now. They'd become more progressive as they'd gone on and Isaac was right on with that: Prog was the future.

'They must have come in when I went back to the dressing room, ' Isaac said.

'I didn't see anybody,' the Void's drummer, Terry said.

'Sneaky bastards,' Isaac muttered. 'What am I going to do now?'

'I can maybe lend you some money, man.' Keyboard Jeff had said. 'My mum's had a Premium Bond win and she said she'll share it.'

They had just been playing in a room in a pub on the Commercial Road supporting a band who didn't pay the support, but felt they were doing The Void a favour by letting them perform.

'I can't take your money, Jeff.'

'Well, you know mate...' Jeff was a kind soul.

'Something'll turn up, mate.' Terry said.

They dropped him off near home.

Isaac got really low over the next couple of weeks. He had no sax so he went to a couple of band rehearsals, but felt totally useless. The Void had a gig in a pub in Lambeth which he went to as part of the audience, and then one later at Elephant and Castle which he didn't even bother going to.

It was Autumn. The clocks changed and the nights grew dark. Isaac got a job helping out the stores bloke at a firm just back of Oxford Street. He did a few extra hours for the cash, but once he'd paid for his board and lodge he still did not enough to buy a sax. He found himself on Denmark Street, London's own Tin Pan Alley. There were offices of music publishers and musical agents in the buildings dotted along. Isaac had a milky coffee in the Giaconda Cafe. He saw Bill Wyman in there, and David Bowie was also known to frequent the Giaconda when he was in town.

The night was gathering. Because the clocks had fallen back an hour, there was the lovely dusk when the shop windows were lit, shining like golden caverns out into the dark street. Isaac finished his coffee, closed the door behind him with the ding of the cafe bell and stepped out. It was cold. He pulled his coat tighter. There was even a fog starting. These were a rarity now since the clean air acts; once the deadly yellow fogs had killed thousands with their mixture of damp from the river and pollution from ten thousand factories; nitrogen and sulphur infiltrating the air like alchemist assassins. Isaac laughed: that would be a good title for a space rock song. He even began to work through possible saxophone riffs as he walked along in the thickening mist. Then he remembered he didn't have a saxophone. Time to go home

Cars edged past him in a long shuffling train, trying to nudge their way onto Charing Cross Road down Denmark Street ahead of him.

A music shop he didn't recognise caught his eye. Classic Musical Instruments. He thought he knew all the music shops in London, but he hadn't seen this one. In the mist wreathed gloom, the lights shone out of its windows. He thought it looked a little antique in style, but there in pride of place was a gleaming, golden saxophone. If his eyes didn't deceive him it was an antique Buescher True Tone in gold plate from the classic age of Jazz.

Wow! What would that be worth now? He went and pressed his nose almost up to the glass and felt the cold as he marvelled and coveted the instrument they had on display.

He stood a long time thinking how much he'd like the sax, and how little he could afford it. Then, when he'd had enough breaking his heart, he almost turned to rejoin the London night, but before he stepped away, the shop door opened and a dark-haired man grinned out. 'Like what you see?'

'Sure,' Isaac said. 'Just can't afford it.'

'Come on in, take a look.'

'Shouldn't you be shutting up by now?'

'Hey, that's my problem. Don't you worry about that.'

The guy must be desperate to make a sale. Maybe he was down on his daily take, but he didn't realise that he wasn't going to get a sale from Isaac. 'Listen, mate, I'm just wasting your time.'

'It's my time to waste,' the man said. 'Just come on in.'

Isaac sighed. He was only going home anyway.

He expected the shop to be warmer, to feel a cushion of warm air as he stepped in from the cold of the street. But it was neutral. It wasn't cold, but it wasn't warm. It wasn't anything. And exactly in line with what he'd thought from outside, it was very old-fashioned. Isaac figured they must be going for a period look. There were no electric guitars, just pianos, woodwind, saxophone, some drum kits, violins and a double bass. As he looked around, he thought they were a jazz specialist. There were piles of old sheet music and some antique looking gramophone records. They must be worth a bob or two.

'So what took your fancy?' the salesman said. They were the only two in the shop, no surprise at closing time of course.

Isaac indicated the gleaming saxophone in the window.

'Ah, that! You have good taste my friend.'

There was something about the bloke that seemed very familiar. The way he talked, his body language and his hand gestures, but, even after furrowing his brow while he tried to recollect who the man reminded him of, he failed. He took the saxophone from the salesman's hands.

'I can't afford it,' he said.

The salesman laughed. 'No, it is a choice item. But if you love the sax, then you need to try it.'

'Try it?'

'Sure, give it a go.'

Isaac hesitated. He felt the cold weight of the saxophone in his hand. It was a beautiful thing. The man waited. Isaac felt almost shy. Then, with a shrug he put it to his lips.

He played the saxophone piece from *April in Paris* by Charlie Parker. He played it well. The sax flowed like honey and molten light; it was smooth, it was sweet and the notes sailed and tripped round the music shop. The salesman stood, grinning and when Isaac had finished. He broke into a round of spontaneous applause. 'Well, son,' he said. 'You have a rare talent. And that sax suits you.'

Isaac liked performing and he liked when people liked his performance. He didn't know why he'd played a famous jazz piece — maybe it was the shop theme and surroundings. He wanted to play something more modern. He played the sax from Children of the Sun. The salesman gave a polite clap when he'd finished. 'Don't know that one,' he said. 'But you played it well.'

'It's a lovely instrument,' Isaac said, making to hand it back.

The salesman didn't take it though.

'Honestly,' Isaac said, 'I can't pay for this.'

The salesman looked thoughtful. 'Listen, son. We get a lot of people come in here and try out our instruments. Some of them are good. Some of them not so good. But you have a phenomenal talent.'

Isaac blushed. 'It's the instrument that makes me sound good.'

'Well, that helps. But if you don't have the talent to start off with, you can't fake it.'

'Very kind of you to say so,' Isaac said, handing the saxophone back, but still the salesmen declined to take it.

'How about it if I lend it to you?'

'What?'

'Well, you can't afford it now, but playing that sax, your future is bright. I see you being a big success. When you make your money, come back and pay me for it.'

'You can't be serious.'

'I am serious. I respect your talent. I know you have a great future. Consider it an investment.'

Isaac looked at the saxophone in his hands. It was beautiful. He wanted it. It was like he'd just been given something seriously magical. He was tempted, but he really couldn't afford it.

'Don't give it to me back. I won't take it.' Seeing that Isaac still hesitated, the man said, 'If it makes you feel better, I'll let you pay me double what it says on that ticket.'

Isaac gulped. The ticket said enough, never mind double. But that somehow made it easier to accept.

'Okay, I'll pay you double. I promise. By when?'

The man grinned. 'I know you'll do well, but let's say maybe a year and a day?'

'A year and a day today? That's a deal.'

The man shook his hand. There was something awfully familiar about him.

'This is really generous of you,' Isaac said.

The man laughed. 'Just think of it as me taking an interest in your career.'

Isaac left the shop with the saxophone in its old-fashioned case. He couldn't believe his luck, but he wouldn't take the mick, he'd pay the guy back — double like he said. Once he made his fortune.

TWO DAYS LATER, HE TOOK THE SAXOPHONE ROUND TO HIS grandmother's house and played for her in her small front room with its net curtains and old-style sofa and chairs.

'Oh, you're so talented!' she said. 'It's lovely.'

Isaac knew Prog Rock wasn't her thing so he played When the Saints and John Brown's body. She kept saying, 'Play me another!' And then the neighbours banged on the thin wall that separated the houses.

'You take after your father,' his grandmother said. 'You've got his talent. He was a musician.'

Isaac went quiet. They never talked about his dad. His mother had brought him up a single parent in South London with help from her parents. Because his mother and father never married and he was born illegitimate, it was a scandal.

'What did he play?'

'Well, I only met him two or three times. But he played the piano. He was a professional. She met him when he was playing one of those dance halls.'

'What happened to him?' Isaac asked quietly. He didn't want to push it too hard in case the flow of information dried up and his grandmother said no more. He knew his mother would never talk to him about his dad.

'He was killed. He was on the M1 heading north to do a concert with his band. They had a crash.'

Anguish ripped through Isaac. 'Why does mum never talk about him?'

His grandmother smiled sadly. 'Too painful. It broke her heart. She never wanted another. She was a pretty girl; she could have had her choice, but none was the equal of her piano player man. You look just like him though.'

His mother told him a little about his father. He was called Dave Butler, a Londoner, but she couldn't remember the name of his band.

. . .

SOON, ISAAC'S THOUGHTS OF HIS FATHER TOOK SECOND PLACE. HE went back to *The Golden Void* and rehearsed and gigged with them relentlessly. He threw everything into his musical career. They got a manager who got them gigs around London and then they had a brief appearance with *Hawkwind* and *Man* at the Roundhouse and Isaac got to meet his hippy idol, Nik Turner. He jammed with Gong one time and things went up and up until they were supporting Yes at the Hammersmith Odeon and then the big break came when they did a few dates backing Genesis for their London shows.

They got a record deal with United Artists by the end of summer and cut their first album *Masks of Poseidon* at the Landsdowne Studio for United Artists. It got to number thirty-two in the album charts which was pretty respectable and they got a hit single off it: *Infinite Staircase*. And the money flowed in.

AUTUMN CAME AGAIN. THE WEATHER GREW MORE CHILL. THE leaves in Kennington Park turned yellow and gold and fell in heaps across the paths, cleared up by uniformed park keepers every morning.

It was the anniversary of him getting the saxophone. The anniversary and one day. Isaac headed into Central London. He had his prized saxophone in its case and his cheque book. He was going back to the shop on Denmark Street to pay his dues. He had to meet the band's manager first on Wardour Street and he took them all for lunch at the Gay Hussar, and Isaac lost track of time. It was getting dark that October night when Isaac began to hurry to Denmark Street. He hoped the shop wouldn't shut early. He hadn't phoned ahead. It even crossed his mind the shop guy might think he would never see Isaac again and now regretted his hasty generosity.

Just like a year previously, it was cold and dark, and the first tendrils of fog gathered as he turned onto Denmark Street. It was like the evening conspired to recreate the conditions of a year ago. He walked

quickly down the street but when he got to where he clearly remembered the shop being, it wasn't there.

The shopfront was gone and the windows now had blinds on them.
The brass sign said it was a musician's agent now. Damn, what if he'd gone
out of business in the meantime? Isaac felt sick with guilt, not that him
paying for the sax would likely have kept the business afloat. He stood
back and looked at the windows. There was light on inside. On impulse he
knocked on the door, then he saw there was a bell so he pushed that too.

A young woman came to the door, holding it ajar. 'Do you have an
appointment?'

'No, I was just wondering how long you've been here?'

She looked taken aback. 'Me? What do you mean?'

'No, the company.'

'I don't know. A good few years now.'

'Years?'

'Yes. Will that be all?' But before he could answer she shut the door
in his face.

That didn't make sense. He knew he'd been there exactly a year and
a day ago. He looked around. The rest of Denmark Street looked the
same as it always had. He hadn't specifically been here he thought in
the past year, but he'd been nearby. He hadn't noticed the shop, Classic
Musical Instruments, but he hadn't been looking out for it.

The Giaconda was still open. He went for a coffee and placed his
saxophone on the table. His cheque book was still in his pocket ready
to pay for it.

The man who served him in the cafe wore a white apron. He was
fat with curly grey hair and looked like he spent a lot of time smoking.

Isaac said, 'Hey, have you been working here long?'

'Who wants to know?' the man said.

'Just that agency down the road.'

'Which? There's tons. They're like rats in a squat.'

Isaac reeled off the name.

'Him? He's a tosser.'

'What was there before that?'

'He's been there ages. Before him there was a sheet music shop.'

'Do you remember there was a shop called Classic Musical Instruments?'

For the first time the fat man's face broke into a smile. 'Yeah, Dave used to run that. He was a top geezer. That was nearly twenty years ago. I was just a kid then. He'd always help me out with a few quid if I was short.' He shook his head. 'He died you know.'

'How?'

'Car crash. He was in a band. They was on their way to a gig. Tragic it was.'

Isaac's heart pounded.

'What did they call him?'

'Dave, like I said.'

The man thought for a while, then with a smile of remembrance said, 'Dave — David Butler, that was him.'